The Next Girl

&

Other Lesbian Tales

TAWANNA SULLIVAN

Published by tpsulli publications
Cover Design by James, GoOnWrite.com

ISBN: 978-0-9984327-2-4

"The Souvenir" © 2003 originally appeared in Hot + Bothered 4: Short Short Fiction on Lesbian Desire (Arsenal Pulp Press, 2003; "The Homecoming" © 2006 originally appeared in Longing, Lust, and Love: Black Lesbian Love Stories (Nghosi Books, 2006); "The Getaway" © 2007 originally appeared in Iridescence: Sensuous Shades of Lesbian Erotica (Alyson Books, 2009); "The Next Girl" © 2007 originally appeared in Purple Panties: An Eroticanoir.com Anthology (Strebor Books, 2008); "Operation Butch Ambush" © 2009 originally appeared in Best Lesbian Erotica 2009 (Cleis Press, 2009); "Just Desserts" © 2009 originally appeared in Swing! Adventures in Swinging by Today's Top Erotica Writers (Logical-Lust Publications, 2009); "Cat and Mouse" and "The One Who Got Away" © 2010 originally appeared in Life, Love & Lust (LM Inc, 2010); "In Remembrance of Her" and "Losing Michelle" © 2011 originally appeared in Life, Love & Lust 2011 (LM Inc, 2011); "Famished" and "Witness" © 2013; "Should Have Seen It Coming" © 2020

DEDICATION

To Martina: thank you for letting me bounce ideas off you.

CONTENTS

Introduction 1

Just Desserts 3

The Souvenir 21

The Getaway 25

Operation Butch Ambush 35

The Next Girl 55

Famished 73

The Homecoming 75

Cat and Mouse 87

The One Who Got Away 107

Witness 123

Losing Michelle 125

In Remembrance Of Her 147

Should Have Seen It Coming 163

Introduction

A collection of previously published stories, **The Next Girl** is an eclectic mix of black lesbian fiction. These are stories of love, lust, desire, mystery, and revenge—with a touch of humor here and there.

There are two stories of "pure" erotica; sex is the engine driving the plot. In *The Souvenir*, a woman riding the subway gets a front row seat to a live sex show. In *Just Desserts*, the erotic potential of chance comes into play when a couple is stranded in the airport.

Several tales delve into the up-and-down nature of relationships. When Narcia loses her lust interest to her best friend in *The Next Girl*, long held resentments rise to the surface. After a disastrous day, lovers in *The Getaway* take an impromptu trip and reaffirm their commitment to each other.

In *Losing Michelle*, a horror writer wishes her partner would leave her alone—until the woman goes missing. Originally published under the pseudonym Evelyn Foster, *In Remembrance of Her* finds a woman negotiating with dark forces in a quest to save her lover. Despite the rumors, Chante is drawn to the mysterious Diana in *The One Who Got Away*.

Themes of community and forgiveness are also explored. In *Operation Butch Ambush*, rival factions come together to save women from a nefarious group that reprograms butch lesbians who have strayed from strict gender roles. Aria comes home from a hellish week at work to a nasty surprise in *Cat and Mouse*. In *The Homecoming*, it's a funeral that prompts Melanie to revisit the past and her fractured relationship with her family.

Also included are flash fiction pieces with bite. *Famished* and *Witness* are about different forms of hunger.

Spanning a decade, these pieces reflect the political and social realities of their times. For example, before same sex marriage or civil unions, a lesbian couple who wanted their union recognized in some legal capacity could get into a domestic partnership (if their municipality offered it).

I enjoyed writing these stories; I hope you enjoy reading them.

Tawanna Sullivan

·

Just Desserts

"Don't worry," Peri said. "In a few hours, we will be back in our own bed and this disaster will be a fading memory."

Cru closed her eyes while her girlfriend massaged her temples. "Whose idea was it to have a family reunion? Your relatives would put a Tyler Perry movie to shame."

"I thought that staying in a hotel instead of with my parents would shield us from the drama."

"Ha!"

Grandma Rose had insisted that both Uncle Mason's ex-wife and his current, estranged wife be invited to the reunion "so that all of the kids can meet each other and the rest of the family." No one told Mason and the fool showed up with his pregnant mistress. That was the touchstone that set off a week of drama. Peri had spent most of the time playing peacemaker. As soon as one situation calmed down, someone else would get their feathers ruffled.

When she wasn't handing out tissue, Cru tried to

stay far away from the group therapy sessions, which meant she spent a lot of time outside with the men. Except for a lecherous cousin who had to be put in his place, the guys were okay. However, she never wanted to talk about barbecue or sports ever again.

Peri leaned over and her breast threatened to spill out of the tank top. "Don't worry," she whispered. "I'll make it up to you."

Though they weren't closeted, Cru had struggled all week to keep her hands to herself—lest the less accepting family members be freaked out by a kiss. Even now, she fought the desire to reach out and stroke Peri's luscious brown curves. "I'm fine," she said. "You are the one who needs to relax."

Just then, the airport shuttle pulled up. It was empty, so they took the prime seat up front. Cru thought she would have time for a quick catnap, but the driver had other ideas. "My name is Rebecca and you girls are my first pick-up this afternoon. Did y'all enjoy your stay?" She was an older lady who almost disappeared into her uniform. In an ideal world, she would be in some retirement village sipping mint juleps while a hunky attendant rubbed Ben Gay into her ankles.

"Yes, ma'am," Peri said, the southern accent front and center.

"Down here for business or pleasure?"

"Family reunion."

"It's nice that you girls come back to see your family. My sister and I can barely stay in the same room." Cru looked at Peri and rolled her eyes, but Rebecca didn't notice. "Hope you come back soon. We really do need the tourists to keep coming in."

Not one to favor silence, the driver continued, "Times are hard for us down here. Jobs are disappearing, there's that foreclosure mess—it's getting so that people will do almost anything for a dollar. Take the Westin Diplomat; it used to be one of our nicest hotels. Guess who had a convention there this week? Swingers!" She waited a beat. "You know, those people who swap wives and have orgies."

Peri perked up. "Oh, really?"

Rebecca nodded. "When something like that becomes acceptable down here, you know we are really living in the last times. After the swingers, it's some porn people. Now, tell me who's going to stay at the hotel after that? I wouldn't feel comfortable there."

"It wouldn't make a difference to me. People have sex in hotels—that's not unusual." The conversation had suddenly turned boring and Peri slipped on her earphones.

"You don't understand. Those people ran around stark naked and … and left nastiness everywhere. Those poor maids have to clean everything."

Cru finally decided to chime in. "The swingers probably haven't done anything that others haven't done first." She put an arm around Peri. "We've had sex on the sofa, in the shower, on the counter of the kitchenette. That's just regular hotel behavior."

From time to time, Rebecca stared at them in the rear view mirror but didn't say another word for the rest of the ride. As they were getting off the bus, Cru tossed a five-dollar bill into the tip bucket.

Peri shook her head and laughed. "You ought to be ashamed of yourself. Were you trying to give the lady a heart attack on the freeway?"

"What? Rebecca may have been disgusted, but she didn't refuse the tip." Cru flagged down a skycap. "Besides, with a mind like hers, she still probably thinks we're sisters."

"Eww!"

After doing the boarding pass-bag check-security shuffle, they were at gate 28 waiting for permission to board the plane. The customer service rep announced bad weather in the Northeast was causing delays. Peri bought some magazines and Cru struggled to find a comfortable position for a nap.

Three hours after their scheduled take off, Cru had a stiff neck and the waiting area had started to resemble a refugee camp. She stood up and tried to stretch the kinks out.

"I'm glad you're awake." Peri pointed to her lifeless iPod. "My battery is dead and I've read the latest gossip on Brangelina twice."

"Fine, I'll keep you company. What's the latest news?"

"The weather is so bad that they aren't allowing any planes to travel in the Northeast."

"We're never getting back home."

"In other news, I spotted a couple with a Westin Diplomat shopping bag."

Cru surveyed the miserable crowd. "Where? Rebecca would be scandalized."

"Gate 27, second row, third seat from the left. The Halle Berry lookalike."

Cru's eyes settled on a beautiful, honey-brown woman. "Hmm. Is she with the dude on the left or the gorgeous sister on the right?"

"You mean Iman—that's what I've nicknamed her. Yes, they are together."

Iman whispered something to Halle and they both smiled. Peri smiled back and nodded. "While you were scaring children with your snores, I've been making eye contact. You don't mind, do you, honey?" She gently raked her fingernails across the back of Cru's hand.

"Of course not." The touch had sent a jolt through Cru that made her tingle from head to toe. Flirting came second nature to Peri and it had led them into all sorts of adventures.

A familiar voice rang through the loudspeakers. "Ladies and gentlemen, we want you to know that we do appreciate your patience. In a little bit, we will be distributing a snack and bottled water."

"This doesn't look good." Peri got up. "I'm going to speak to one of the reps. An airline giving away anything is not a good sign." She returned about ten minutes later, clutching her cell phone. "The plane sitting at the gate isn't ours. Our plane hasn't left Newark yet—and it's not going to."

"Our flight has been cancelled?"

Peri nodded. "Word came down while I was at the counter. They'll be announcing it soon. I've already called the travel agent. We're booked on a seven a.m. flight to Baltimore. I figure there are hundreds of people trying to get to Newark, so we'd be better off renting a car and driving the rest of the way."

"That's fine. I'll drive, but you have to make sure something decent is on the radio."

A few people noticed that the word "cancelled" had replaced "delayed" on the flight monitors and the crowd became agitated. The counters were swarming with angry customers.

Cru's stomach flip-flopped. "Now that they've

mentioned food, I'm starving. A bag of chips isn't going to be enough. I'll treat for dinner."

They got to Chili's Too in time to get the last free table. The waitress took their drink order and disappeared into the crowd. Peri took a cursory glance of the menu before tossing it aside. "We should have gone over and introduced ourselves."

"We don't know that they were actually at the convention." Cru shrugged. "We're not even sure they are a couple. They could be sisters or something."

"Now you sound like Rebecca."

"What was your plan? Stroll over there, point to the bag, and say, 'So, ya have a good week?'" Cru leaned forward and was winking and gesturing wildly.

"We had a fabulous time, but it would have been even better if you were there." There they were— Iman and Halle in the flesh. It was the dark chocolate Amazon that spoke. "I'm Mona and this is my partner, Erica. We decided to swing by and say hello." It was corny, but it broke the ice.

Peri didn't miss a beat. "I'm Peri and this is my

partner, Cru. Please join us for dinner."

Erica was the one with the suspicious shopping bag. "Are you sure? We don't want to impose."

Cru found her tongue again. "It's no problem. We're stuck here for a while, might as well make friends."

"We like making new friends." Mona sat next to Peri. "I take it you ladies are trying to get back North. We're from Albany. Where do you call home?"

"Jersey City. We're practically neighbors—give or take a couple of hours." When Peri passed a menu to Mona, her fingers lightly grazed the woman's forearm.

The waitress came back and was very perplexed by the new faces at the table. "Do you two want something to drink too? Let me get you a couple of menus."

"No need," Cru said before the woman vanished again. "Everyone is ready to order now."

They chatted and flirted through salads and light appetizers. Peri loved being the center of attention. Mona and Erica were clearly under her spell.

Cru sat back and watched the three interact. Away from the not-quite-in-laws, she was finally free to look at women and see sensuality bubbling just underneath the surface. Erica's nipples had hardened and, every time she breathed, part of a tattoo peeked from under her satin shirt. Mona liked talking with her fingertips. She could hardly get out a sentence without touching a forearm or caressing the back of a hand. Peri's eyes always sparkled with mischief, as if she knew your most secret kinky fantasies and wanted to help fulfill them.

It was Erica who asked the question that had been lingering in the air. "So, do you two like to play?"

No one had actually asked outright before and Cru found herself fumbling with the answer. "Yes, but not in any kind of formal way. We don't go to parties or anything like that."

"But," Peri added, "if we are at a club and the mood is right, we may not go home alone."

After exchanging a glance with Erica, Mona licked her lips and smiled. "We've booked a room at the airport Holiday Inn and you're welcome to join us. We can order dessert, watch a little television, relax, and you won't be more than ten minutes away from the terminal."

A wicked smile spread across Peri's lips. "What do you think, Cru?"

"I think you deserve a sweet treat."

~

It was a nice room with a queen-sized bed, a sitting area, and a kitchenette. Mona kept her word about dessert and it was not long before room service appeared with hot fudge sundaes draped with extra whipped cream.

Peri had slipped off her shoes and got comfortable in the recliner. She winked at Cru and then looked at Mona. "I want your cherry."

"Watch this," Cru whispered to Erica.

Mona took a cherry, made sure it was drenched in cream, and dangled it just above the goddess' lips. Peri's tongue wrapped around the fruit and took the entire piece into her mouth. In less than a minute, the stem re-emerged tied around the pit. There was applause all around.

Cru felt Erica's nose nuzzle against her ear. "That

was impressive, but what kind of tricks can you do?"

Goosebumps shot up her arm and the sundae Cru was holding tilted too far to the left, spilling warm sticky sauce on her pants. "Fuck!" Rubbing it with a napkin didn't help. "I'll take care of this and be right back." She went to the bathroom, stripped off her jeans, and tried tackling the stain with a washcloth and soap.

"You aren't supposed to rub a stain." Erica sat the lopsided sundae on the sink, took the cloth, and began blotting the stain. "Rubbing only makes it spread and pushes it deeper into the fiber." Then, she pulled a stain removal pen from her pocket and the dark spot all but disappeared.

Cru was suitably impressed. "Now, that is a neat trick."

"I have two kids; there's not a stain around that I haven't mastered by now." Erica took a step back and admired the shapely form before her. "I didn't figure you to be the type to wear boxers."

Looking down, Cru realized that she'd thrown on the pair that had a gigantic smiling face over the slit. "They just feel good, you know. Give the

illusion of not wearing any underwear at all."
Maybe it was the bathroom light or the awkward
silence, but Cru began to sweat. "Look. Peri usually
plays and I like to watch. Seeing her cum is so
amazing. She's so beautiful—"

"What?" Erica's voice was thick with
disappointment. "Well, if that's what you want to
do, let's see what they are up to."

"No, wait. I'm just saying that's what we usually
do." She sighed. "I feel like a teenager again—and
that's not a good feeling."

"I make you nervous? I'm not going to bite. Just
tell me what you like."

Cru let her fingers drift to the hem of Erica's
shirt. "What I'd like is to see the rest of that tattoo."

"You noticed it, huh? I knew you were checking
me out at the restaurant." Erica took off her top and
leaned against the doorframe. On her abdomen
were two dragons that formed a heart. Their
intertwined tails disappeared under the skirt.

"This is amazing." Cru got on her knees to take a
closer look. Twisting her hips, Erica let her skirt
and panties fall to reveal it all. The tails melding

into a crisp arrow pointed to the top of her bush. "Did it hurt?"

"One person's pain is another person's pleasure. Besides, it's a great incentive to stay away from carbs."

Cru pointed at the ice cream. "What are we going to do with all of this ice cream?"

"Just because I'm through, doesn't mean you can't enjoy it." Erica took a spoonful and let it dribble down her stomach.

Cru met the river of chocolate as it rolled past the dragons' tails. As she rose to lick and suck the trail of sweetness, she caressed Erica's calves and cupped her firm ass. The bra hooks were released and a few seconds later, the breasts were completely free. "That's my trick."

Erica braced herself as Cru gently dipped her breasts into the bowl, but the shock of cold made her shout. Then, Cru's mouth set to cleaning up the new mess and paid extra attention to the cream-covered nipples. Erica gently pushed her away. "You better be careful or you'll get chocolate all over you."

"That's exactly what I want." Cru nearly tore off her shirt and shorts. "You all over me."

Scooping the last of the cream on her fingertips, Erica let Cru suck them dry. "Now give me a taste." They wrapped their arms around each other and began kissing. Tentative at first, their tongues and limbs intertwined.

Cru reached back and turned on the shower. "Let's clean up, so we can get really dirty." The bathroom was filled with giggles and laughter as they lathered each other up.

"Assume the position." Erica turned Cru toward the tiled wall and made her spread her legs. Reaching around, she palmed and squeezed her nipples while nibbling the back of her neck. "Are you still shy, baby?"

"No," Cru managed to whisper between moans.

"Good." Erica backed up under the water and put her leg on the side of the tub. "I hope you're thirsty."

Cru crouched down and watched the droplets of water slide against her glistening clit. Her tongue gently explored the delicious folds. She curved her tongue around the clit and sipped at the rivet of water cascading from it.

Erica gripped Cru's shoulders, holding her in position while she rode her face to the pinnacle of pleasure. She wasn't prepared to feel the tip of a tongue darting into her opening and lost her balance when the force of the orgasm pushed her back. Cru had wrapped her strong arms around Erica's torso and wouldn't let her fall.

After drying off, they tumbled out of the bathroom and fell across the bed. Erica pulled Cru on top of her. "You're going to have to take another shower. You can't get on a plane smelling like hot cream."

"I said I wanted you all over me and I meant it." The unmistakable sound of a hand smacking against flesh reverberated throughout the room. "It sounds like someone out there is getting a good spanking."

"Want to watch?"

"How?"

Erica dimmed the lights and opened the closet door. When she got the angle just right, the mirror inside gave them a perfect view of the sofa. Peri was bent over the arm while Mona alternated between spanking and fucking her.

Peri was radiant. Her breasts were free and bobbing with the rhythm. Her eyes were partially closed and Cru knew that she was in her space. Anything could set her off now—a feather stroking her arm, a gentle breeze blowing against her back, hot breath against her ear...anything.

"Get on your knees," Erica whispered. "Not all the way up. On all fours. Yes, like that." Lying next to her, she reached up to play with Cru's clit. "Don't look down at me or I'll stop. You don't want me to stop, do you?"

"No." Cru wanted to clamp down on the fingers inside of her, but she stayed perfectly still.

"You watch her. I want to watch you."

Erica matched Mona's tempo and Cru felt herself losing control. She tried focusing on Peri but, when their eyes met, Cru gave in to the joy spreading through her body like a wildfire. She collapsed and Erica pulled her close. 'You are beautiful when you cum too."

The Souvenir

It happened the night of Rita's birthday party. After everyone else left, I stuck around to help her clean up. We didn't get through until about four a.m. Rita offered to let me stay on the sofa, but I'm not afraid to catch the subway at night.

I caught the P local at the Reed Street Station. It was a cold five-minute wait for the train, but I got an entire subway car to myself. At least, for about the first three stops. Then, at Forest Station, this dark chocolate beauty stepped in. She had a short, curly brown afro with honey-blonde streaks and her breasts strained against a low cut, sheer blouse. I lowered my gaze to her thigh-high, black leather boots, which ended just at the hem of her mini-skirt.

I was just starting to admire the perfect curve of her ass when another woman walked in after her. It was obvious they were a couple. Wearing black dress pants and a polo shirt, the girlfriend looked like she had stepped out of the pages of *GQ*.

Now, with all the space available, these two sat directly in front of me. Honey was practically sitting in her girl's lap. They were whispering and stealing peeks at me, but I was determined to ignore them. I had totally blocked them out, until a low, sensuous purr caught my attention. GQ had a hand up Honey's blouse and was kissing her neck. The moans were coming from Honey. She was biting her lower lip but looking straight at me.

Suddenly, Honey's breasts were fully exposed and freely swaying with the movement of the train. Turning her back to me, Honey straddled GQ's legs and began rubbing against her. GQ pushed up the mini-skirt, revealing a supple booty barely contained in a black thong. "Yes, baby, fill me up," Honey said, her moans interrupted by little cries of pleasure.

My nipples were throbbing and my pussy was a damn waterfall. I wanted to be GQ. I could just imagine pushing the thong aside and my fingers being sucked in by Honey's pussy. I'd rub her clit with my thumb while tickling her g-spot and nibble on her nipples as she bucked against me.

I wanted to cross the aisle and plant little kisses all over Honey's back. My tongue would trace the contours of her spine and delve into the cleft of her ass. Instead, I rocked back and forth, savoring the sensation of my lips sliding against my clit.

Honey slid off of GQ's fingers and nearly lost her balance as she sat on the bench. GQ got down on her knees. Draping a leg over each shoulder, she buried her face in Honey's pussy.

Bracing herself, Honey winked at me. "That's right, baby. Suck it. Isn't it juicy?" She began writhing and twisting, but her eyes never left mine. "I'm ready to come for you, baby. Just for you—" Suddenly, she arched her back and her gasps and screams echoed throughout the car, empty except for us three.

GQ immediately stood up and gathered Honey in her arms. They cuddled and kissed for a moment and then Honey started dressing. My pussy was quivering. All my clit needed was one good stroke.

When the train pulled into the Liberty Street Station, they rose out of their seats. Honey wriggled out of her cum-soaked thong and dropped it in my lap on her way out.

Of course, I kept it.

The Getaway

This trip to the country was impromptu. Sarah had come home from the police station, literally thrown some clothes into her gym bag, and was riding shotgun. Nicole's foot was heavy on the accelerator, and it wasn't long before Baltimore was a distant blur in the rear view mirror.

They rode in silence until they lost the frequency for their favorite easy listening jazz station and a steady stream of overdubbed bass poured through the speakers. Sarah turned off the radio and finally exhaled. "Thank you for this. I just needed to get away from there."

Nicole nodded, never taking her eyes off of the road. "It's no problem. My aunt owns a bed and breakfast in Brockburg. I let her know we're coming. Are you okay?"

"Yeah."

"Are you sure? It was bad enough finding Michelle's body, but I didn't think the police were ever going to let you go."

Sarah winced as she remembered the gruesome

discovery. She had gone to the theater directly from church and found her ex-girlfriend with her head pushed into Maggie's litter box. Someone had knocked Michelle unconscious with her precious Vagi, an award for best performance in a lesbian-themed one-woman play, and left her to suffocate in the ammonia-stenched hell. The killer had hit her so hard that the little silver clit had fallen off of the statue and rolled into the orchestra pit.

"It was terrible. The police think I only pretended to find the body. According to a note found in Michelle's pocket, she was supposed to meet some mystery person at 11:30. They think I slipped out of service during offering, killed her, and then magically appeared back at the organ in time for Sister Franklin's solo."

"I'm sure there were at least one hundred witnesses who will testify that you never left service." The women at Mt. Holy Redeemer always kept too close an eye on Sarah for Nicole's taste. It was amusing at first to see the female members of the young adult choir looking hungrily at their director with their lips and legs always parted just enough to invite temptation. There was a fine line between adoration and nuisance; hormone-addled youth crossed it every time.

On second thought, Nicole really couldn't fault them. When talking to Sarah, it was quite easy to find your gaze slipping from her eyes and resting on her bosom. Nicole took a quick look over at her beloved. The tears had stopped and the chest no longer heaved, but fully erect nipples threatened to poke through her cotton tank top. Was she excited or was this just some weird biological response to stress?

Sarah thought Nicole was taking a side-eye glance of her legs and shifted them accordingly to give a proper view of her thighs. "They say I have the strongest motive. She ruined my credit and threatened to out me to my boss, but I have better sense than to kill her before rehearsal."

"Don't take it personally." Nicole reached over and patted a newly available knee. "I'm sure the police interrogated the rest of the cast. Some cop gave me the third degree when I showed up at the theatre looking for you."

"Yeah, they talked to everybody. It just looked so bad that I arrived first. Damn me for being punctual." Actually, the police were interested in her because she had said something outrageously stupid: *I was surprised that she was dead but not disappointed.* It would have been a cute throwaway line in a comedy. Baltimore law enforcement was not so easily amused.

In fact, Detective Campbell had suggested she not leave town. That was why this jaunt on the open road was so exciting—she enjoyed being a bad girl. Instinctively, her fingertips grazed Nicole's forearm while she daydreamed about them fleeing the scene like a modern day Bonnie & Clyde. *We can get away with this*, Sarah thought.

"What's the status of the play now that the director is dead? I imagine Little Ms. Ride My Hood will be a hot ticket. The whole production can be in her memory."

"I don't know. We still need a lot of work and I don't know if Karla, the assistant director, can whip everyone into shape. You should have seen Lynette go into hysterics when she found out Michelle was dead. She didn't fool anyone."

"Are there other suspects or do you definitely think it's someone from the show?"

"Half the lesbian population of Baltimore hates— hated Michelle. She knew how to play on your sympathy with that poor starving artist act. So dedicated to her craft that she couldn't afford the luxury of having a steady paying gig. When the money dried up, she moved on to the next patron."

"Did you know about her reputation before?"

"Yes and no." Sarah ruffled her fingers through her locks to hide the flush of embarrassment making its way across her cheeks. "There were some rumblings overheard here and there, but you expect that from ex-girlfriends." A memory from the morning resurfaced and she had to fight a fit of nervous laughter. "Poor Maggie was standing next to her litter box, meowing at Michelle's head."

"Try to put that behind you. I've got some things in store that will help take your mind off it."

"Like what? Cow tipping?" After another stretch of quiet, Sarah got tired of counting cows and cornfields. "What time is it?"

Nicole glanced down at her empty wrist and shrugged. "Want to stop and stretch your legs for a minute?"

Sarah nodded and they pulled over at the Wicomico River scenic overview. Except for where waves lapped at the banks, the river appeared as calm as a lake. The valley beyond was a patchwork of different farmlands and crops.

Nicole sat on the trunk of her Impala and pulled Sarah into her lap. "Clear water and fresh air. This would have been a nice spot for a picnic."

Gray clouds had rolled over them and brought a soft, spring shower. "A soggy picnic." Sarah leaned back and drew Nicole's arms around her. "This feels good, though." Lips brushed against the back of her neck and sent a tingling ripple throughout her body. "Nic, don't start something you can't finish."

"Who says I can't finish?" Nicole caressed her shoulders and kissed her collarbone.

Sarah tilted her head to the left, giving full access to her earlobe. "Not out here; someone could see us."

A squirrel darted out into the landing, shrugged at them, and disappeared into a cornfield. "I don't think he's going to tell anybody."

Sarah studied herself as a hand found its way under her skirt and between her thighs. When fingers reached the entrance of her hot, pulsating center, she reached back and grabbed a handful of Nicole's braids. "Wait," she whispered. "I need to tell you the truth. To confes—"

Fingers alternated between stroking her inside and spreading her juices all over her clit. Between quakes of pleasure, Sarah fought hard not to lose her train of thought. "I tampered with the evidence." In that one moment, everything stopped. Hands retreated. No more cool kisses on hot skin. "Nic, I—"

"Sh." Nicole leaned back and watched raindrops land and drizzle down her lover's back. Maybe this was just part of a game. Sarah always liked to bring a bit of her acting class into the bedroom. Nicole bent her forward and pulled up her skirt. Then, she unzipped her pants and let her dildo rest against the newly exposed booty. *Okay*, she thought, *let's play.*

Sarah was relieved to feel Delilah pressed against her, but the slap that followed caught her completely off guard. Fear mingled with excitement and she found herself quickly approaching the edge of orgasm. It had been so long since she'd been properly punished.

"You little slut." Each word was punctuated with

stinging spank. With years of Catholic education under her belt, Nicole knew how to deliver strokes without leaving marks. "Did you promise Michelle pussy? Lure her there . . ."

"No!" Sarah spread her thighs and Delilah slipped and slid across her lips. "That's not what happened."

"Why?" Nicole whispered. "Why did you do it?" She pulled Sarah upright and squeezed her nipples. She pulled them roughly as Delilah bounced rhythmically against her clit.

"You. I took it to protect you."

Sarah tried to say more, but her words dissolved into moans. A hard bite on the shoulder tipped the tide of passion and her knees began to buckle. She felt lightheaded, as if her soul was rising up in a bid to flee, but it couldn't escape. It was then that Delilah finally slipped inside of her and set off an explosion that rippled through every inch of her body. Sarah heard herself crying . . . felt them both collapsing against the side of the car . . . sinking into the soft, rain-drenched grass.

Nicole was dumbfounded. She had been so careful: picking a time when she knew Sarah would have an unshakable alibi, wearing gloves once she got inside the theatre, discarding her clothes to get rid of all traces of litter and cat hair. "Sarah, I'm sorry. You weren't supposed to know."

Sarah rolled over on top of Nicole and kissed her. "It's okay, baby." She pulled a gold watch from her pocket. "The clasp is broken, but I'm sure we can get it fixed in Brockburg."

Sunlight had returned and glistened in Nicole's tear-filled eyes. Sarah kissed them. "Don't worry, baby. I'm going to take care of everything."

Operation Butch Ambush

Hip-Hop Soul night was in full swing at The Blue Gator. From her place at the bar, Charlie could take in all of the action on the floor and survey the new women filing in. It didn't take long to find a target. They began an intricate eye tango: stare, lock eyes, smile, look away, repeat.

During the third round, Charlie noticed that her Coke had dwindled down to ice cubes. She turned to flag down the bartender. A few minutes later, she felt a hand on her shoulder. The young Latina woman demanding her attention was in full Mack Daddy gear, from her snug fitting baseball cap to her freshly pressed jeans.

Though she was scowling, there was no real menace in her voice. "Stop staring at my girl. We came out to have a nice time. Why you got to be disrespectful?"

Charlie took a sip of her refreshed drink before responding. "And you are?"

"Anna."

Charlie looked over Anna's shoulder at the lady

in question. Her overly painted face was a mixture of pride and embarrassment. "How would she know I was looking over there, if she wasn't looking over here?"

Anna turned the scowl up a notch. "Back off, okay?"

It could have ended here, but Charlie was feeling mischievous. "If you came all the way over here to defend her honor, you wasted your time."

"What the fuck are you trying to say?"

"Let's not play this game." Charlie put her glass down. "You know I was looking at you."

"Hell no!" Anna looked dumbfounded. "You ain't got no business looking at me like that. Do I look like some kinda femme to you?"

"Even the hardest woman has a soft spot and I want to play with yours." Charlie gently caressed Anna's forearm.

Stepping back, the young stud almost knocked a drink out of someone's hand. "I don't know where you come from—"

"Charlie. I'm Charlie."

"—but we don't do that butch/butch stuff up here." Anna struggled to find the right words. "That's just too gay."

"Well, you don't have anything to worry about because I'm not a butch."

Five minutes later, they were in the back of Anna's Jeep. "We're not supposed to be doing this," she whispered as Charlie nibbled on her earlobe.

"If you feel uncomfortable, tell me to stop."

Once Charlie's lips found their way to the sweet valley between her neck and shoulders, Anna's inhibitions melted away. She unbuttoned her denim shirt and allowed access to her pierced nipples.

Charlie pulled and twisted the silver rings with her teeth. Discovering the bulge in Anna's jeans, she began to gently tug it. Anna moaned as the strap-on rhythmically rocked against her clit.

Before Anna could protest, Charlie had unzipped her pants, unsnapped two of the leather clasps of the d-ring, and was directly strumming her clit.

Then, the phone rang. Charlie would have ignored it, but it was Toi's ringtone. Reluctantly, she drew back. "Be chill, sweetie. I have to take this." By the time she got to the phone, the ringing had stopped, but she had a brand new text message: *My house-15min-Toi.* Anytime Toi was home on a Friday night, something had to be wrong. Either El had managed to get arrested again or Denny had returned from her latest straight-girl escapade with a broken heart.

Anna had come back to her senses and was hurriedly trying to fix her clothes. The dildo didn't want to snap back in place, so she kicked it under the driver's seat. "Don't tell anybody about this shit, okay?"

"I won't." They exchanged numbers and Charlie gave her another kiss before heading back to her car.

~

Latoya "Toi" Bennet, Elsa "El" Sparks, Denise "Denny" Franks, and Charlene "Charlie" Boyd were the original Fierce Fucking Four. It was a silly name they had given themselves after their ouster from the Butch/Femme Preservation Society. Their motto was simple—no matter whom you find yourself attracted to, be fierce enough to admit it and act on it.

As word got around about how much fun they were having, others wanted to join in. Since four had grown to over twenty, a new name was in order. Playbois, Hardy Bois, and Lost Bois had all been suggested and thoroughly ridiculed. Since all the meetings were held at her house, they'd settled on Toi Bois for the interim.

Charlie recognized the motorcycle in Toi's driveway and felt her blood pressure rising. It belonged to Ruth Carson, president of the Butch/Femme Preservation Society. When Ruth began purging undesirables from the group, she hadn't expected Toi to leave with the expelled. She was obsessed with bring the wayward femme aggressive top switch with a bondage fetish back into the fold.

Ruth was on the sofa fidgeting with a cup of coffee. Charlie immediately went on the offensive. "What the fuck are you doing here?"

"Stand down, soldier." Toi greeted her with a kiss and steered her towards the recliner. "I know this is awkward, but we need to put our personal issues aside." After Charlie settled into the chair, she continued, "You know the show *Butch Ambush*?"

"Of course, I do." Charlie rolled her eyes. "A so-called lax butch gets snatched off the street and offered $10,000 to take a week of butch lessons from gracious hosts Rocky and April."

"Some contestants have disappeared." Toi turned to Ruth. "Tell her about the BRC."

Stripped of vitriol, Ruth's normally boisterous voice was flat. "They haven't actually disappeared. When you sign the contract to appear on the show, you basically enroll in the Butch Reformation Institute and agree to stay until you are a fully functioning butch. If Rocky and April aren't satisfied with your progress after the first week, you get sent to the Butch Re-education Center. If a femme tries to raise hell about her missing girlfriend, the Butch Ambush lawyers come out in full force."

"So," Toi cut in, "if you don't conform, you don't go home. Police are useless because, technically, no one has been kidnapped."

Charlie picked at a loose thread on a pillow cushion. "Ruth, I think you're full of shit. On the off chance that everything you say is true, it still doesn't explain why you're here."

Averting Charlie's gaze, Ruth ran a hand through

her salt and pepper locks. "The BRC is actually the basement of the Butch Ambush studio. We have an ally on the staff, but security is very tight. We need you and Toi to pose as applicants, get inside the building, and raise hell. While you are the center of attention, our agent will help us break in."

Her patience wearing thin, Toi was more direct. "Ruth thinks there is a spy on her team."

"We've tried to send decoys before, but they were turned away at the gate. No one knows that I've come to you and I've tapped a few trusted friends for the raid." Finally, Ruth couldn't resist a dig. "Besides, you're the perfect candidate for the re-education center."

"Fuck off, Ruth." Charlie went into the kitchen. Instantly, she was upset with herself for letting the old bulldagger's words sting. She felt better when Toi's cool lips brushed against the nape of her neck. "I still think this is a setup. Since when do couples apply together to be on the show?"

Toi gave her a hug. "That's the way it works, baby. The ambush is just a theatrical way to start the show. No one is really surprised when that van shows up."

Charlie thrust her hands in her pockets. "I'd feel better about this if we could get the rest of the bois involved."

"Letting anyone else know about this collaboration beforehand could jeopardize it." Taking out her compact, Toi refreshed her mascara. "After they finish with the butches, who do you think they will ambush next?"

"Fine, I'm in."

~

"A producer will be out to speak with you in a few moments." The receptionist took their application and smiled at them. "Three others couples have already been in today, but I think you two really have a shot." She buzzed them into the lounge.

Charlie wasn't sure they could pull this off. Ruth hadn't exaggerated about security; they had to go through two metal detectors and a pat down to get in the door. Hidden by a dense wood, the building itself was completely surrounded by an electrified fence. It was the perfect place for some crazy cult to take its last stand.

Toi pulled Charlie close and began playing with her ear. "Don't be nervous," she whispered between nibbles. "You are Diana, I'm Tara, and we're just here because we need that ten-thousand-dollar prize money to go on a cruise."

Taking the hint, Charlie relaxed and tried to get in character. "Easy for you to say. No one is talking about fixing you."

"That's because I'm perfect."

A mousy-looking production assistant appeared with clipboards for them. "Your applications aren't complete," she said. "Neither of you signed the waiver."

That was no waiver. It was three pages of archaic language written in miniscule print. "We'd have no problem signing the waiver if we were actually chosen for the show," Toi said. "After our attorney has vetted it."

The woman was visibly shocked. "You can't move forward in the interview process—"

"I think we can make an exception in this case," said a husky voice from behind. It was Rockalene Shea, the host and executive producer of *Butch*

Ambush. Next to her was April Gorey, the femme half of their production team. The pair began circling Charlie like hungry sharks. "Sister," Rockalene began, "you look like you've lost your way. Tattoos and piercing everywhere—you look like a perpetual beach bum. Is that makeup?"

Since Rockalene looked like a football player turned mortician, Charlie decided not to take the criticism personally. "I like following my own path."

"Are you really following a path or just letting the cards fall where they may?"

"I bet she doesn't open doors for you," April said to Toi. "Does she cater to you or does she take your femininity for granted?"

"We do all right," Toi responded.

April put a sympathetic arm around her. "But that's just it, sweetie. If you wanted to settle for just all right, you wouldn't be here."

Toi sighed. "I guess."

The production assistant cleared her throat. "Okay, then. You will have one-on-one interviews with Rocky and April. If they decide to take on the

44

project, we will need to get your signatures."

Charlie was ready to follow Rocky into the hallway when the elder stateswoman shook her head. "I know deep down inside you are eager for some of this wisdom, but I'm interviewing Tara. She needs to learn how to recognize a good butch when she sees one." With a grand gesture, she offered Toi her arm and escorted her away.

"Come on, Diana," April said. "I get to give you a full evaluation and suggest a course of treatment."

"Whatever you say, Dr. Gorey." On their journey, Charlie made note of the restroom and utility closet.

The tiny office actually looked more like an interrogation room. There was a desk, two chairs, and a small window overlooking the trash compactor. The worn folding chair creaked and groaned as Charlie tried to find a comfortable position.

They spent the first few minutes in silence while April pored through the application. Occasionally, she stopped shuffling papers to make notes. "I see you two have an open relationship. You don't mind if someone else fucks Tara?"

Charlie grinned. "Nope, and I don't mind if she fucks someone else. Not everyone is meant to be monogamous."

"Why are you really here, Diana?"

"For the money, of course."

"Do you really need money?"

"T wants to go on this cruise—"

"Do you want to go?"

"Well, I don't really—"

"So, you let your girl bully you to get a makeover you don't want and go on a cruise that you don't want to be on."

Charlie shrugged. "People who love each other compromise."

"And what has Tara ever given up for you?" April didn't give time for an answer before going in for the kill. "You are spoiling her—and that's not what she wants. A femme doesn't want to run roughshod over her butch; she needs boundaries. She wants to be put in her place."

Examining the scuff on her sneakers, Charlie

appeared to be in deep thought. Ruth had briefed them on the pitch April used to suck in potential contestants. "T wouldn't see it that way."

"Maybe not consciously, but she did turn you in." April switched to a more sympathetic tone. "Let us help you become the woman she needs."

"Whatever. If she's not satisfied with me, she'll tell me. Y'all can ambush someone else."

"Now, your girl would be pretty upset if you walked away from this without even trying. It's just seven days."

"Okay. What would it take for you to reject our application, to tell Tara that I don't qualify for butch lessons?"

April partially drew the blinds and sat on the desk. "Tara's application says that you need to learn proper table etiquette." She opened her legs to reveal a well-coiffed pussy. "Let's see if you can eat this sweet poontang without making a mess."

This wasn't in the script, but Charlie didn't hesitate. "No."

The femme hostess extraordinaire frowned. "Don't tell me. You're the type that can't fuck without some false extension of manhood?"

"I didn't say I wouldn't fuck you." Charlie retrieved a safe sex kit from her back pocket and snapped on a purple glove. "I'm just not going to eat you, no extensions needed." She put April's left foot on her shoulder. Gentle tongue strokes made the tightly toned legs tremble.

A salty-sweet aroma greeted Charlie as her cheek glided along April's thigh. Spreading open the glistening lips revealed a fat little clit that had thrown off its hood. She stroked it gently with her gloved thumb. "Do you like that?"

"Yes," April whispered between labored breaths.

A chill went through Charlie's body as manicured nails raked lightly through her short afro. Pulling April to the edge of the desk, she stood up to relieve the pressure on her own throbbing clit. "Hold on tight, baby. You're about to go on a ride." The thumb didn't break its stride as one and then another finger slid into the eager pussy.

Now, face to face, it was evident that the femme taskmaster had disappeared. The new April was radiant and vulnerable. "You feel good," she said.

She pushed the straps of her dress down and, arching her back, offered her newly exposed breasts.

Charlie's tongue flicked over the hardened nipples as she massaged April's walls with slow, measured strokes. Legs wrapped tightly around her waist. Suddenly, April's quick breaths turned into moans.

The quivering started at Charlie's fingertips. Charlie watched, entranced, as the waves of orgasm quietly spread out to the surface. Fighting the impulse to scream had forced tears from April's eyes. With one last shudder, she went limp. "Don't move," she whispered. "Please."

"So, do you still think I need lessons?"

"No." April said before laying her head on Charlie's shoulder.

Charlie was awash in sexual energy. She wanted to drop her pants and rock her clit against April's lavender painted toes. Instead, she gently lowered April to the desk and announced she was going to the bathroom. Thankfully, no one was there to see her scramble out of the room disheveled. Summoning the image of Ruth was enough to put her own fire out and get back to the business at hand.

Before putting the second phase of their plan into action, Charlie checked in with Toi. She walked into Rockalene's executive suite to find her sitting behind a large mahogany desk. "Girl, you should have knocked," Toi said. "I was ready to hurl this phonebook at you." She pointed at the purple glove and smirked. "So, did you handle Ms. April?"

As much sex as she'd had in her life, Charlie couldn't understand why talking about it still made her blush. "Yeah, you can say that." She tossed the drenched gloved in Rocky's recycle bin. "What happened to your host?"

Toi pointed at the empty sofa. "She said some stupid shit about wanting to put me between a rock and a hard place."

Charlie found the butch guru on the ground, tied up with phone cord. It wasn't needed—she was out cold. "So you knocked her out?"

"It's not my fault Rocky's got a glass jaw." The computer beeped and ejected a CD. Toi replaced it and clicked the mouse a few times. "I'm copying her hard drive. We need to know everything she knows. Ruth is concerned about her crew, but we need to see the big picture."

"Okay, finish up. We'll be running out of here soon."

Toi waved her away.

According to Ruth's spy, the bathroom shared an air duct with the security office. Charlie's first stop was the utility closet, where she found turpentine and paint thinner. Bolting the door to the ladies' room, she removed the grate over the vent. This time, she put on a pair of gloves and soaked a bunch of paper towels in the turpentine. They were dropped down the shaft first. She poured paint thinner down behind them, making sure it flowed down the sides and didn't splash.

The fumes were giving Charlie a headache. She splashed water on her face before tossing down two lit rolls of toilet paper and her gloves. Though flames had spread quickly through the duct and had spilled over into the bathroom, she walked out as if nothing unusual had happened. An assortment of alarms sounded and the sprinklers came on.

The noise brought both Toi and April into the

corridor. Toi gave Charlie a high five. "Excellent," she said. "Our part is over. Let's get out of here." Then, Toi turned to April. "You better wake your girl up and get her out of here."

April looked from them to the smoke billowing from under the bathroom door. "What did you do? Who are you?"

Charlie blew her a kiss. "We're Poontanganistas, baby! Liberating the world one pussy at a time!" Just then, the lights went out. She grabbed Toi's hand and ran.

Once they were far enough away from the compound, Charlie took out her binoculars. Fire engines had started to arrive and the employees were out on the lawn. In the back, Ruth and friends were leading a group of disoriented butches away from the BRC.

After learning about Operation Butch Ambush, the rest of the Toi Bois were extremely unhappy. El and Denny felt, as original members of the Fierce Fucking Four, they should have been consulted. Several bois hated the idea of helping a rival organization.

Except for reminding everyone that it was a spur of the moment, do or die situation, Toi sat grim faced through the tongue-lashing. By the third round of beer, the conversation had turned congenial and all had been forgiven.

Toi again took center stage. "While Ruth was busting up the BRC, we decided to do a little digital dumpster diving. I haven't parsed all of the data yet, but *Butch Ambush* was just the tip of the iceberg. We may have made a powerful new enemy." She paused to let the statement sink in.

Denny yelled, "I guess we'll just have to keep kicking ass! Who are we?"

"The Poontanganistas," the others cheered in response.

Charlie felt the familiar vibration in her pants and checked her cell phone. The pleasurable tingle had come from Anna. "I think we've got a new recruit."

The Next Girl

Raina is my best friend — and I hate her. We've known each other for over ten years. If there was anyone who would have my back, it would be her.

Everything was fine until Raina started dating my next girl. The next girl is the woman you have your eye on while you're trying to break up with your current girl. Jelisa Friday is a goddess. I'm not just talking about her smooth velvet voice or her delicious chocolate curves. She's the kind of woman who can smile at you and all of your worries just fall away. She's smart, sexy, and should have been mine.

I had been laying the groundwork with Jelisa for a few weeks. I still had love for Stephanie, but things hadn't been working out for a while. Going home to her was like going into a war zone. I had timed it so that the transition from Steph to Jelisa would be seamless.

Now, let me set the scene for you. Stephanie and I are at the Allegro to cheer on one of her co-workers in the Mr. Gay USA competition. The house lights are down low and a dude in a thong is on stage flexing his muscles. Suddenly, Jelisa walks into the room and it's like the whole world stops. Yes, even the men all paused. I didn't hug her as usual—I'm not going to disrespect Steph to her face—but I made space for her at our table. That's when I turned around and saw Raina beside her.

Neither announced they were on a date, but their actions proved it. Throughout the whole evening, there were sly touches on the arm and whispers. Jelisa loved the attention. They barely acknowledged our presence at all. After Mr. Gay USA had been crowned, Raina took her to some dark corner to do God knows what.

I couldn't believe it. My best girl had stolen my next girl and there was nothing I could say about it.

Raina is a notorious playa; no woman can hold her attention for long. So it didn't surprise me when cracks started appearing in their relationship. We were back at the Allegro playing pool. I had just finished a new version of my Stephanie-is-getting-on-my-last-nerve rant, when Raina finally dropped the bombshell. "Jelisa is starting to move a little too fast for me." Then she leaned over and ever so gently tapped the 3 ball into the right corner pocket.

I stepped back, took a sip of my whiskey sour, and nodded for her to continue. "She gave me a set of house keys," Raina complained. "She's expecting me to give her a key too. My mother doesn't even have the key to my place." She tossed down a few peanuts and, with a bank shot, sank the 7 into a side pocket. "Narcia, this girl is talking domestic partnership. I'm just trying to make it to a six-month anniversary."

It was clear that Jelisa was about to get her feelings trampled on and I, Narcia, didn't care. Served her ass right for not being patient and waiting for me.

Since I didn't say anything—hey, I'm not Dr. Phil—Raina kept "processing" her feelings. Shot after shot, she whined about how she was nervous about settling down. "Honestly, I'm not trying to run away this time."

At the end of the game, all Raina had to do was hit the 8 ball into the right back pocket. Anyway, that's the pocket any normal person would have chosen. A few other women had gathered around to cheer her on and she wasn't about to disappoint her fans. She pointed her cue at the front left pocket. "Eight ball in the corner," she announced and everyone oohed and aahed on cue.

When she slid the stick behind her back and winked at me, I looked away in disgust. Next thing I knew, everyone was clapping and Raina had a mini entourage escorting her to the bar.

That was when I started thinking about how Raina never missed an opportunity to humiliate me. She's a better pool player than me, so why the fancy shots? Just because she could. Raina knew how I felt about Jelisa and had no business stepping to her like that. She could have had any girl she wanted, but she had to take my next girl.

As you can see, that shit started eating me up on the inside. The idea hit me on the cab ride home. Why should Raina always have it her way? What if she was the one who got dumped? Even better, what if I stole Jelisa back...

This time was going to be different. I could do it all: get my next girl, make Steph my ex-girl, and burn my trifling best friend. The best part? Raina was going to help me do it.

Every woman, gay or straight, secretly suspects that her lover has or will cheat. It was easy to plant the seeds of doubt. When Raina and I went to a football game, I would sneak out of the stands and make a call. "Jelisa, where's your girl? She was supposed to meet me in front of the stadium a half hour ago. Oh wait, here she comes." Before I got back to my seat, Raina's cell was going off.

During the next round of the pool tournament, I pretended to have a low battery and asked to borrow Raina's phone. I put it in my pocket and conveniently "forgot" about it. Ms. Hustler was too busy performing tricks to realize it was missing. Jelisa had called five times during the night. When confronted, Raina simply told the truth and got chewed out for it.

I didn't see Raina again until Steph decided to have a 70s throwback party. Her vision was to turn the basement into a disco and the first floor into a lounge. I recruited Raina to be the bartender and Jelisa volunteered to help Stephanie with the food. When Raina walked in, I almost didn't recognize her. She used to greet everyone with a smile and a hug. This time, she didn't even look us in the eye. She just nodded her head and stood off to the side. You would have thought she was sick or something.

Steph had prepared lunch for us, but Raina

wanted to get started. It was like she couldn't wait to get up from under Jelisa. We'd just finished putting up the speakers, when the cooking crew announced they were making a grocery run. The door slammed shut behind them and it was like a weight fell off of Raina's shoulders. "Jelisa acts like I'm fucking somebody if I'm out of her sight for two minutes." She popped the caps off of two wine coolers and passed one to me. "Get this, I'm not doing anything. I go from work to Jelisa's house. If I go home to my apartment, she either calls twenty times for nothing or shows up at my doorstep because she misses me. How do I have time to cheat?"

While my best friend was fighting back tears, I had to take a quick sip to stop myself from breaking into nervous laughter. Honestly, I felt guilty. I thought Jelisa would dump her and Raina would feel the sting but bounce back. I offered her some practical advice. "Why don't you just leave her? You've gotten so wrapped up in this chick that you are losing yourself."

"I love her. She wasn't this person when I met her. I want to get the real Jelisa back."

True to form, once the party started, Jelisa was

right at the bar monitoring Raina's interactions. She was like a guard dog, ready to accidentally bump or shove aside any woman who was being too friendly. Everyone knew something was wrong and Steph was two seconds from going off on Jelisa herself.

As usual, it was up to me to save the day. I put on Donna Summer's "Bad Girls," grabbed Jelisa's hand, and forced her to dance. It's like the entire crowd sighed in relief. The whole room was shaking its groove thing.

My boy Carlos took over the turntables for me so I could go outside for a minute. My little polyester suit was drenched with sweat. I was holding a cold bottled water to my forehead when I heard the screen door open and close behind me. It was a slightly tipsy Jelisa. "What are you doing out here by yourself?" she asked.

I thought it was obvious, but I played along. "Trying to keep cool."

"That's not how you do it." She took the water out of my hand, opened it, and took a good, healthy drink. She pushed herself against me; we were so close I could feel her heart beating. Her cool lips grazed my cheek and lingered there before kissing my neck. A cold chill went through my arms and legs, but that triangle between my nipples and my pussy was on fire. The different sensations jangled my nerves and I had to grab the rail to steady myself. Jelisa smirked and went back inside.

Damn, I thought to myself, *she's looking for the next girl.*

There was a change after the party. Jelisa began calling me on my cell just to shoot the breeze. The longer I thought about it, the more my sympathy for Raina's situation faded. If she didn't have enough sense to leave a woman who was treating her bad, it wasn't my fault. Besides, it was time that the scales of fate tipped back in my favor.

Turns out I didn't have the upper hand at all. I was going to the Chambres Shopping Center and cut through the Franklin Square Condo development. It's an exclusive community that has its own security to keep undesirables out, but I knew all of the guards. When Raina was dating Trina, we hung out there all the time.

I had almost made it to the underpass when I ran into Officer Blabbermouth. She knows everybody's business and has no problem broadcasting it. Soon as she saw me, she started grinning from ear to ear. "Narcia, how you been? It's about time you showed up."

"I'm okay. What do you mean?"

"Your buddy is already at Trina's place. Is there a party going on tonight?"

"Yeah, I guess so."

When I finally managed to get away from her, I took a detour to Trina's townhouse. I'll be damned if Raina wasn't walking out of the house. Trina was standing in the doorway pulling her bathrobe closed. They exchanged a few words and then kissed like she was going off to war or something. I looked over at the clock tower. It was 5:30. Raina was working overtime, alright.

Stephanie didn't have dinner ready when I got home, but I was too agitated to eat. Raina was acting like she was one argument away from a nervous breakdown, but she had been phasing Jelisa out. How long had she been talking to Trina? What really fucked with me was that I didn't know anything about it. We were supposed to be closer than sisters and she hadn't said shit to me.

It was really time to knock Raina down off of her high horse, and I wanted her to know it was me who threw the punch. When Jelisa got home from work the next day, she found me sitting on her front steps.

"Narcia? What's up? Did something happen to Raina?"

I took a deep breath. "Something has been weighing heavy on my heart and I've got to come clean about it." Hers eyes welled up as I continued. "You should know what's going on."

A few minutes later, we were sitting in her den and the tears were flowing freely. All I did was tell the truth. "I caught them in the act. They were nearly fucking in the doorway. Raina's hands were all up under that robe. I knew you suspected something, but I didn't want to say anything until I knew for sure."

Jelisa started wailing. "I hate that bitch."

I got a tissue and started wiping her cheeks. "Nah, girl. Don't scrunch up your face like that. You are too beautiful to go into hysterics over anyone." I started stroking her chin and she moved closer to me and put her head on my shoulder.

"I tried so hard," she said. "What's wrong with me?"

"You're a good woman and you deserve better." Now, I had rehearsed this all night, but something unexpected came out of my mouth next. "I should have just gotten rid of Stephanie instead of asking you to wait. None of this shit would have happened if I had treated you with the respect you deserve. I'm sorry."

I meant it too. There was just something about seeing Jelisa weak and vulnerable. I wanted to put my arms around her and protect her from the entire world. Raina had done her dirty, but I was the one who had made her cry.

I raised her chin to kiss her forehead. Then, I was kissing the tears from her eyes. Her lips touched mine… In that moment, it wasn't about Raina, Stephanie, or anybody else. Both of us had an emptiness that needed to be filled.

Her bold move at the party should have been a clue that she wasn't a pillow queen, but I was caught off guard when she pulled me on top of her. I continued kissing her tears away, and she gently raked her nails across my stomach. I was trying to work the buttons on her blouse, but she got my shirt off first and began sucking my nipples.

I tried to pull away, but Jelisa had a damn good grip on my khakis. She was fighting to pull my zipper down. "Let me touch you in all the places your girl won't." Next thing I knew, her hand had slipped inside of my boxers and was massaging my pussy.

When she parted my lips, the hot, sticky pool that had welled up inside of me flooded her fingers and my clit. Jelisa was gently stroking my outer walls, trying to find the way inside. I jerked myself away just as she was about to enter. I felt like I was going to fucking collapse.

I could barely catch my breath. "Nah, babygirl, this is about you."

Slipping down to the floor, I nudged her legs apart. There is nothing sexier than a woman in stockings. When her body is trembling and that nylon is roughly sliding against your tongue, it feels damn good. I swung her right leg over my left shoulder and rubbed my cheek against her thigh. Her essence was intoxicating.

I nibbled my way down to her garter and stopped as she lifted herself to meet me. Jelisa never wore underwear—she made that quite apparent when we first met. My nose nuzzled against her clit and she jumped. "Come on, baby," she begged. "Don't tease it."

We settled into an easy rocking rhythm as I tasted and teased her lips. My tongue had just curled around her clit, when the front door opened.

Bam! I was on the floor. Jelisa pushed her skirt back down, buttoned up her blouse, and went out to meet Raina.

I just sat there stunned. It was the one night Raina decided not to work late. A minute hadn't passed before the shouting began. "I'm tired of you accusing me of shit I haven't done!"

I got dressed, went into the kitchen, and tried to wash the scent of Jelisa from my face. Instead of hiding, I decided to stroll into the living room as innocently as possible. Of course, I picked the worst fucking possible moment. Jelisa was crying again and waving her arms frantically. "You spent the entire afternoon with her."

Raina's voice had returned to normal, but the way her jaw was clenched, you knew she could fly off again any second. "I told you I needed to stop by her house to drop off some paperwork. I got there around four and didn't stay for more than five minutes."

"You left her house at 5:30! Somebody saw you."

"Who?"

"It doesn't make a difference who. You are busted!"

That was when my size nines walked into the living room and they both turned to look at me. Jelisa was still screaming, but my eyes were locked with Raina's. "You're my girl and everything," I said, "but wrong is wrong. I saw you kissing Trina and I didn't think Jelisa should be kept in the dark."

Raina didn't even blink. "You had to tell her in person so that you could be here to comfort her?"

Jelisa didn't appreciate being ignored and stepped right up in Raina's face. "If you had been where you were supposed to be, none of this would have happened."

"Okay, fine." Raina pulled out her cell phone and stepped out on the porch.

I walked over to Jelisa, but she wouldn't even

look at me. "You have soap on your chin," she said.

When Raina came back inside, she put a key on the bookcase. "I don't need this anymore." Jelisa started to say something, but Raina wasn't having it. "You could have at least waited to ask me about it first, but you've been looking for any excuse to fuck my so-called friend, right?"

The tissue Jelisa had been using had disintegrated and she was wiping her running make up with the back of her hand. "Why are you always blaming other people for your mistakes?"

"Let's go for a ride." A smirk slowly spread across Raina's face and she issued a challenge to me. "Come on, Narcia. Why don't you show us exactly what you saw?"

Before I could say anything, Jelisa was back to yelling. "I don't want to talk to Trina. That bitch would say anything for you."

Raina never took her eyes off of me. "No she wouldn't. Besides, I'm not about to drag her into this mess. I just want to show you that Narcia couldn't possibly have seen what she told you."

This seemed too good to be true. Raina wasn't

even fighting to keep her girl, but I didn't appreciate her trying to throw the spotlight back on me. I figured she was bluffing, so I decided to take her up on it. "Jelisa, I know what I saw. Your ex-girl is just trying to save face." Then, I nodded to Raina. "Let's go."

I thought Raina was going to punk out at the last minute, but we were zooming down I-83 before I could button my jacket. She made both of us sit in the back. There were no more tears, but Jelisa alternated between staring at the back of Raina's head and glaring at me.

At night, the Franklin Square area was deserted. We parked on the street and walked to the same corner I had seen them from. I pointed out Trina's townhouse. "See, I have a perfect view. You can see the whole courtyard from this spot."

The fire came back into Jelisa's eyes. "This ain't nothing but some bullshit. Don't waste my time. All the crap you have left at my house will be sitting outside in the morning. It's trash day, so you better get it early."

Raina smiled at me and then turned to Jelisa. "Why don't you ask your new girl what time it is?"

Jelisa was confused. "What? It's 7:30. What does that have to do with anything?"

I looked up at the clock tower. It was still 5:30. I made this gargling sound; words were caught in my throat. That was when Jelisa started screaming at me. She had seen it too.

Raina started laughing. "That clock hasn't worked in months, so it's always 5:30 in Franklin Square."

Jelisa was bawling her eyes out and punching me in the chest. Then, Stephanie's car pulled up. It clicked—that was who Raina had called.

As my best friend drove away, I could feel the gates of hell closing in on me.

Famished

It started when I let Tim have a taste of the chicken cordon bleu. He talked about how lucky I was to have a woman who could cook. His old lady didn't know how to crack an egg. I had to chuckle at that.

It wasn't so funny when he became obsessed with my lunch. Every day, salivating over my beef wellington or eggplant towers—the man was a nuisance.

One day, Lauren stopped by to drop off my wallet and love hit Tim like a cast iron skillet. He grumbled 'bout how a beautiful woman like that deserved better than an old bulldagger.

First came the late night phone calls. Then, Lauren began going out with "friends" I'd never met. Tim stopped looking me in the eye.

When she moved in with him, Tim thought he had scored a coup. Fool maxed out his credit to give Lauren the kitchen of her dreams. Come lunchtime, though, all he has to show for it is watery tuna salad on stale bread.

My ex can't cook worth shit.

The Homecoming

It had taken eleven years, but hell had finally frozen over. It was death that brought Melanie back to the cobblestone driveway of 735 Munson Lane. Not twenty-four hours ago, she had watched her mother's coffin being lowered into the ground.

The stubborn pride that had helped the matriarch raise three children on her own kept her from going to the doctor until the pain became unbearable. Left unchecked, cancer had ravished her body.

Melanie leaned against the steering wheel and watched a slug struggling across the sidewalk. *What am I doing here?* The prodigal daughter hadn't expected to be included in the will, much less to inherit the house she had been banished from.

A car pulled up next door and a gorgeous brown-skinned woman emerged from the driver's side. After a brief struggle, she managed to lift a couple of grocery bags out of the backseat. With her hands full, she couldn't close the door and seemed reluctant to use her khaki-clad hips. Her grip loosened on one of the bags and it started to slip.

Happy for the distraction, Melanie seized the opportunity to be neighborly. "Hey, let me give you a hand." She sprinted across the lawn and took one of the bags.

"Thanks, Melanie." The woman shut the door with her now free hand. Then, she ran her fingers through the sandy-brown locks that framed her face. "You probably don't remember me. It's Wanda."

"Wanda Andrews?" *No way*, Melanie thought as she followed her up to the porch. This curvaceous beauty was a far cry from the shy little girl who wore over-starched dresses and patent leather shoes. "Wow, I can't believe it. It's been about twelve years."

"Are you still living in New York?" Wanda hesitated at the front door and decided to settle into one of the lawn chairs instead.

Hoping none of the groceries were perishable, Melanie followed her lead and sat in the swing suspended from the awning. The cushion was thin and the rusty hinges cried as she sank into them. "No, my wallet couldn't take it. I moved to

Delaware a few years ago."

"Sorry about your mother. How have you been holding up?"

"It was a shock, but I'm okay."

"How long are you staying?"

"I'm not sure. Mama left the house to me."

"Are you serious?" Her eyes danced with delight, but Wanda suppressed her smile. "How did your sister take it?"

"It was the first time I've ever seen Gloria speechless. It lasted all of thirty seconds. She began talking about home inspections and how much she expected from the sale."

"You're going to sell the house?"

"Probably. There's nothing really for me here."

Suddenly, the front door jerked open. Her wig slightly askew, the elder Andrews pressed her nose into the screen door. "I thought I heard voices out here. Wanda, why didn't you let me know you were back?"

Wanda shifted uncomfortably. "Ma, we didn't

want to disturb your afternoon nap."

Motioning towards Melanie, Mrs. Andrews lowered her voice. "Who's this? One of your friends?"

"No, Ma. Remember Melanie from next door?"

Melanie smiled. "How are you doing, Ms. Andrews?"

"Can't move around like I used to, but I can't complain. You Vicky's youngest, right? The one who got grown and ran away?"

Ran away? "Well, I—"

"You look pretty good for living out in the street. How many babies you got?"

Now Melanie understood why she hadn't been invited in. "None." The older woman looked unconvinced. "I lived with my brother for a few months and got a college scholarship that let me move on campus."

"Well, you should thank God for that. Maybe you can talk some sense into this one."

"Ma!"

"Got a little education and she think she grown."

Wanda jumped to her feet. "Ma, Melanie just stopped by to help me with the groceries. She has to get back next door to help Gloria pack some things."

Huh? Melanie thought. A look from Wanda told her to keep quiet.

"Vicky ain't been in the ground long enough to get cold yet and y'all picking over her stuff like vultures. Wanda, don't you let that happen to me when I die. You watch Hattie Mae around my jewelry." She clicked her false teeth in disapproval. "Hmph, that fiend is liable to take the gold tooth out of my head."

"It was good seeing you again." Wanda gave Melanie a quick hug. "Run before she starts asking more questions," she whispered.

The scent of lavender engulfed her and Melanie thought she was going to melt in Wanda's arms. She reluctantly let go. "Come over if you get a chance. It would be nice to catch up on old times."

"I'd like that."

Melanie held the screen door open while Wanda

took the bags into the house. "Nice seeing you again, Mrs. Andrews." The old lady slammed the door without looking back.

Wanda had been a nice little detour, but it was time to face the inevitable. Melanie stepped over the thin rail that separated their porches. She took a deep breath, unlocked the front door, and went inside.

The odor of stale cigarettes and beer greeted her in the foyer. It was dark, but she easily navigated around the end tables and chairs to the picture window. Pulling back the heavy drapes flooded the room with sunlight. Almost nothing had changed. Melanie felt like she had stepped back in time.

Victoria could never bring herself to throw anything away, so the living room was cramped with furniture. The end tables had a new coat of varnish, but one of the St. Bernard lamps had lost its paw. A newer television sat atop a broken, antiquated floor model. Bric-a-brac shelves were nearly overflowing papers and trinkets.

Half-empty cups and paper plates were strewn across the sofa and tables. The gathering may have started somberly but had probably ended in family reunion mode. Once the alcohol had started flowing, they probably stopped crying and started trading scandals and secrets.

Melanie wasn't in any of the photos that lined the faux fireplace mantel. It was likely that she had been exorcised from the family album too. She was a phantom confined to the realm of family gossip.

Closing her eyes, Melanie took stock of her feelings. She thought returning would stir up old pain and rage. It was a relief to know her fears were unfounded. There was no anger, just sadness.

Continuing into the dining room, she realized the china closet was empty. The only dishes left were in a box on the table. Next to it was a list of furniture & household items Gloria had claimed as her own. Damn.

Melanie turned toward the kitchen, but the bag of garbage sitting in the entryway was an ominous sign. The last thing she wanted to confront was a sink full of dishes. As if to save her from the dilemma, the doorbell rang.

Wanda was leaning over one of the dehydrated plants, giving Melanie a full view of her assets when she opened the door. Her neighbor had certainly filled out nicely. "My mother cultivated killing plants into a high art form."

"With a little loving care, anything can be revived." Wanda straightened up and brushed the dirt from her hands. "I hope this isn't a bad time?"

"Oh, no. Please, come in." Wanda walked in, leaving the scent of lilacs in her wake. Melanie quickly cleared the sofa of debris. She hoped the dark patches on the cushions were part of the design and not a sticky spill. "I have to warn you, this place is like an exterminator's wet dream."

"Don't worry about it. Housekeeping is the last thing that should be on your mind."

When Melanie sat down next to her, she could have sworn Wanda edged a little closer. "You know, I was pretty impressed with you back there. When we were kids, you couldn't tell a lie to save your life."

"I didn't know any better back then. As soon as you were out of earshot, she told me to find out who was getting your mother's housedresses."

"Your momma is a trip. You still live next door?"

"I live in Washington Village. It's just far enough to keep her from dropping by unannounced."

"I'd offer you refreshment, but I don't trust anything in that refrigerator. Have you had lunch? I can order us something from Loon Ye. They are still in business, right?"

"About three years ago, Loon Ye changed from a carry out to a real sit-down restaurant. He bought out the stores next to him—"

"The cleaners and the thrift store?"

"Yeah. It's now called Shanghai Delight. The food is the same, but now you are paying for ambiance."

"Sounds like property values have gone up. That's why Gloria is in such a hurry to put a for sale sign on the lawn."

"All of this just got sprung on you. How are you really handling it? "

"Honestly? I'm not sure. We still weren't on speaking terms when she passed, so there is this weird aura of unfinished business. On the other hand, if she were still alive, I couldn't imagine us reconciling anytime soon. She—we— were a little too stubborn for that."

"Maybe leaving you the house was her way of welcoming you back home."

"Part of me really wants to believe that. It's more likely she did it to get back at Gloria." Melanie took a deep breath and shook her head. "How could it have been so easy for her to expel me from her life?"

Wanda put a reassuring hand on her shoulder. "I don't think it was easy, but she was too proud to admit she was wrong."

"I want to be over it and I'm fine most of the time. It not as sharp as it used to be, but the pain is still there."

"There's something I need to tell you." Wanda tensed up and pulled away.

The sudden change in tone put Melanie on guard. "What's that?"

"It's my fault you got thrown out."

"What are you talking about?"

"I told your mother that you liked girls. I was jealous of all the attention you were giving Lisa."

"Lisa Jenkins?" Melanie's mind flashed back to the athletic girl she had been infatuated with for a summer.

"I had no idea she would disown you. I'm sorry."

"Listen, it wasn't your fault. I left her a thousand clues, so the confrontation would have happened anyway. Kicking me out of the house was her choice. Nobody else can take responsibility for that."

"I thought Ms. Vicky would make you come back to church and we could sit together like we used to."

"So, you had a crush on me, huh? I had no idea you felt that way. Good thing too. I probably would have ended up hurting your feelings anyway."

"You think so?"

"I was a bundle of hormones ready to do anything with any girl. On top of that, I didn't even know how to kiss. Thankfully, I've learned a few things since then."

"Have you?"

Before Melanie could offer a demonstration, her cell phone rang. She rolled her eyes when the number appeared on screen. "Hold on." Putting a hand over the phone, she whispered, "It's Gloria."

Wanda's lips brushed against her ear. "Are you hungry?"

Melanie tried to calm the flurry of butterflies in her stomach. "Ravenous."

"Good, I'll make a reservation at Shanghai Delight." Wanda settled back and whipped out her own phone.

Melanie turned her attention back to her sister. "What's up, Gloria? Cancel it; I'm not ready to meet with a realtor yet." Her fingertips traced the outer curve of Wanda's thigh. "I'm going to stick around for a little while and see what develops."

Cat and Mouse

The wind and rain beat a frantic rhythm against the car and the windshield wipers fought a losing battle. Aria should have pulled into the rest stop and waited out the storm, but home was only sixty miles away. While most of her co-workers were stuck at the airport, she would have the privilege of sleeping in her own bed.

It had been a hellish week. The new CEO had decided to take the annual management retreat in a radically new direction. Workshops and leadership building had been replaced by a mishmash of new-age spiritual whole-being-ness and customer manipulation. Marketing gurus hired for the week tried to convince them that they were spiritual partners, not indistinguishable cogs in the corporate machine.

In whispered conversations, everyone acknowledged it was a waste of time—stockholders are not going to hold your hand and meditate for higher dividends. Anyone who spoke out in-session was accused of being negative. Aria sat in the circles, took her turn with the ceremonial "speaking stick," and tried to act the part of a true believer. Fake smiles, fake community, fake intimacy—she couldn't wait to get away from those people.

Home was sanctuary.

A truck surged past and Aria struggled to keep control of her Jeep. Tightening her grip on the steering wheel, she crept around accidents and suspicious pools of water.

The relief Aria felt as she pulled into her own driveway was immeasurable. She decided to leave her suitcase in the trunk; if a thief was desperate enough to risk the deluge for her dirty socks, then more power to him.

A few steps on the cobblestone path and she was at her front door, searching for the right key. It seemed like an eternity to get the locks open. Then, she was greeted by a rush of foul, nauseating air. "Damn!"

After taking a moment to collect herself, Aria took two steps into the living room, turned on a lamp, and collapsed on the sofa. The screen door was no match for the storm, but a damp rug was a small price to pay for fresh air. Her shoes and socks were drenched. She pulled them off and, as if on cue, a black lump of fur appeared to purr around her naked ankles. "What have you done, Mr. Scissors?" she asked. "Turned the whole house into a litter box?"

Mr. Scissors had a knack for ignoring criticism. He rolled over on his back and exposed his fat belly. She scooped him up—he definitely hadn't missed a meal— and held him close. "Mommy missed you too. She's just pissed that no one bothered to scoop your poop."

Aria thought back to the night before she left. She had wanted to leave Mr. Scissors in a cat hotel, but her best friend Rachel was appalled by the idea. "That's cruel! How would you like to be ripped away from home and locked away for a week?" Other people in the restaurant turned to see what the fuss was about and Aria wanted to disappear into the floor.

Even a brochure from the place couldn't convince Rachel that Mr. Scissors would be in the feline version of a country club. "I would let him stay with me, but..." Rachel didn't have to finish. She was taking care of her sick mother and barely had time for herself.

That was when Jennifer, Rachel's girlfriend, volunteered for cat duty. "I can stop by in the afternoon and make sure he's getting plenty of food and water. I'll play around with him for a little bit." Though she was talking to Aria, Jennifer had reached across the table to stroke her lover's hands.

Rachel was thrilled with the idea and, against her better judgment, Aria had given Jennifer a set of keys.

She sighed. "And now I have a house full of shit."

Slowly beginning to recharge, Aria glanced around the room. From the books spilling off the shelves to the cat toys piled in the corner, everything looked just as disorganized as she left it. If Jennifer had been snooping, at least she had been nice enough to put everything back in its place. It was great to be in familiar surroundings.

She noticed new claw marks in the recliner's wooden handle. The scratching post she had strategically placed next to it still looked brand new. "What am I going to do with you?" Mr. Scissors ignored her and began washing his face. He was innocent, of course. "Let's see what other damage you've done."

Aria pushed herself up and started towards the kitchen. The plan was simple: empty the litter box, open a few windows, take a hot shower, and then bed.

In the dining room, Aria was surprised to find the litter box nestled in its usual corner and practically empty. Mr. Scissors made a point of strolling over nonchalantly and lying in front of his throne. His tail gently swept the floor and brought her attention to a few smears of dried blood.

The smears led to bloody paw prints that were more pronounced as her gaze followed them into the kitchen, past bowls overflowing with cat food, to a small clump of brown and red sitting on the linoleum. "Congratulations Mr. Scissors, you've caught a mouse." At least she hoped it was a mouse and not one of the many rats attracted to the vacant house next door.

It wasn't until she flipped on the light and looked around the counter that Aria discovered the "mouse" was a ponytail and attached to a woman's head. "Rachel?" She touched the shoulder and the neck tilted unnaturally backwards to reveal the soulless eyes of a stranger.

Concern transformed into terror and Aria

whirled around to make sure no one was behind her. She ran until she felt the cold, muddy ground under her feet.

It was after she heard the wail of the first siren that she realized the rain had stopped.

~

"Baby, this was a great idea." Rachel took Jennifer's hand as they left Brasserie Bordeaux. "I miss having one on one time with you." It had taken a leap of faith to leave her mother in the care of David, her baby brother, for the night.

"Reservations be damned. I knew we wouldn't have a problem getting a table." Jennifer's black Corvette pulled up to the curb and the valet made a point of opening the door for each of them. "Now that the body has been fed, come home with me so I can feed your soul."

Throughout dinner, Rachel had tried to silence the pangs of desire welling up within her. She had failed miserably. "Let me call home just to make sure everything is all right."

Pouting made Jennifer look like an exasperated five year old. "If there was an emergency, David would have called the restaurant and he has my home number."

"I'll turn the phone on to see if he called. If he hasn't, I'll turn it back off." Rachel didn't want to argue. Lately, what little time they could carve out together ended in anger and hurt feelings.

"Do whatever you have to do to put your mind at ease. Tonight I want you all to myself." Jennifer drove away from the restaurant entrance, but there was no reason to get back on the highway until she knew which direction they were going in. She knew she was treading on thin ice. Rachel had warned her from the beginning that she couldn't dedicate herself one hundred percent to a relationship.

The series of short beeps from the cell phone indicated that a voicemail message had been received. Rachel had to listen to it three times to fully comprehend Aria's trembling voice: *There's a corpse in my kitchen.*

Jennifer didn't even try to hide the irritation in her voice. "What's wrong?"

"We have to go to Aria's house."

"You haven't seen her for a whole week. One more day won't hurt."

"She said there's a dead woman in her house." Aria's line was busy, but Rachel kept hitting the redial button. "Was everything okay when you saw Mr. Scissors this morning? Did you lock the door behind you? Of course you did. Someone must have broken in." Her partner's silence troubled her. "Everything was fine this morning?"

Jennifer rested her head against the steering wheel. "Fuck," she whispered. "I couldn't make it to Aria's on Tuesday. I was supposed to go after work, but half of the office is on vacation and clients were having problems left and right. "

"Why didn't you tell me? I could have fed the cat with no problem."

"How? Were you going to run halfway across town to take care of him on your lunch break? I asked Maria to check up on him."

"Maria?" Rachel shook her head in disbelief. "The intern from last year?"

"I was going to get the key back from her tomorrow. Did Aria say how it happened?"

"No. We won't find out sitting here. Let's go."
Rachel needed a distraction and began a fruitless
search for a decent radio station. There were too
many questions lingering in the air. This wasn't the
right time for jealousy—especially if the girl was
dead.

"Baby, I'm sorry." For her part, Jennifer noted
that Rachel had stopped worrying about her
mother.

They drove the rest of the way in silence.

~

Aria leaned against the trunk of her car. She
stayed out of the way of the procession trudging
back and forth into her house. She clearly, though
not calmly, told the 911 operator that the woman
was dead, so why did the paramedics bother
showing up at all? Though her feet were still cold,
at least she was wearing shoes now. Tucked safely
away in his cat carrier, Mr. Scissors hissed at
everything that moved.

Two officers had questioned her already. Now
Detective Fox, a weary looking man in a crumpled
suit, was taking his turn. "Ms. Temple, do you
know the deceased or have any idea why she's in

your residence?"

"No."

"Is anything missing?"

"I don't know. I ran out of the house and haven't been inside since." It was the first time Aria had seen a body outside of a casket. She tried to cleanse the image from her mind, but it wouldn't budge. "She didn't look like a thief." Detective Fox raised a bushy eyebrow. "I mean, she was wearing a business suit."

"We can look into that later. How long has the body been here?"

Aria tried not to show her frustration, but she sensed he was trying to trick her. "I don't know. I've been at Greenfield Lodge for the last eight days."

"For business or pleasure?"

"Business. It was a management retreat."

"There was a flood warning in this area. Any reason you had to risk life and limb to get here? Were you meeting someone?"

"No." Her one-word answer led to furious

scribbling in his note pad. She should have called a lawyer too. "I just wanted to be back in my own bed."

"According to her license, the deceased is Maria Alvarez. Doesn't ring a bell?"

"No."

"Can you explain why she had a key to your house?"

"No."

The screen door opened and two men brought the body bag out on a stretcher. The detective left her in the driveway and met the coroner on the porch. Aria clamped her eyes shut and fought the urge to be sick.

"Aria, are you okay?"

She turned to see Rachel and Jennifer walking towards her. Dodging Rachel's embrace, Aria turned the full force of her anger to Jennifer. "What the hell did you do?"

Before Jennifer could answer, Detective Fox returned. "I have some good news for you, Ms. Temple." His words had lost that accusatory tone.

"Coroner suspects the deceased had a seizure and hit her head on the counter. We won't be certain until an autopsy is completed, but it doesn't look like homicide."

"Detective Fox, these are my friends Rachel and Jennifer." Aria nodded towards the couple. "Jennifer is the one who volunteered to cat-sit for me."

The word "volunteered" got the eyebrow excited and the detective gently led the now sobbing Jennifer aside to get a statement. Rachel started to follow them, but Aria blocked her path. "What do you know about this?"

"Jennifer couldn't make it every day, so she asked a former intern to feed Mr. Scissors. I didn't know this until a few minutes ago."

"An intern?"

"I know. I don't think she knew the girl all that well."

When Aria saw Jennifer coming back to join them, she crossed her arms. It had been decades since she'd been in a fight, but she didn't trust herself not to put her hands around the woman's throat. Jennifer dabbed her puffy eyes with tissue. "Aria, I'm sorry. I didn't have the time to come every day and I didn't want to put more of a burden on Rachel."

"I entrusted you with the keys to my house. Not Rachel's house. I should have been your primary concern."

"I know what I did was fucked up."

"You don't get it. This is not about you or your feelings or what you want or what you were trying to do."

Rachel touched Aria's arm. "It's unfortunate that she died, but—"

"No, I'm tired of you defending her." Aria pulled away from her friend and months of animosity came to the surface. "Flirting with women in front of you, pressing you to put your mother in a home—dismiss all that if you want to. I'm not going to pretend that she didn't give a stranger the key to my house."

Jennifer backed away and said to Rachel, "They want me to go to the police station and give them a full statement. I'll wait by the car."

Rachel couldn't look Aria in the eye and her voice was barely above a whisper. "Do you have anywhere to stay tonight?"

"I'll be okay. Get your girl out of here before there's a real murder."

~

It had taken two weeks, but Aria was finally starting to feel comfortable in her own home again. After delivering the news that Maria Alvarez's death was the result of internal hemorrhaging brought on by a self-inflicted skull-fracture, Detective Fox had given her the number of a trauma scene clean-up service. They had come in their big blue suits like they were working with radioactive material. Even afterwards, she thought a faint odor of death lingered. It had taken a top-to-bottom scrubbing by a maid service to give her nose comfort.

Her boss was horrified and told her to take all the time she needed. A kinder, gentler workplace did have its merits. Mr. Scissors had ended up going to the cat hotel anyway while she stayed at her cousin's house. When they returned home, he ran around inspecting the house. He stopped for a brief moment in the kitchen, sniffed the air, and then bounded down the basement steps in search of mice.

The first few days, Aria couldn't even go near the dining room without replaying the gruesome discovery in her mind. After the third nightmare, she decided to remodel the kitchen and give the entire house a makeover. A late-night "Clean House" marathon had finally convinced her that there was no reason to keep clothes that were two decades removed from the latest fashions. She was in the basement now, packing up clothing and other items she had earmarked for charity.

Mr. Scissors was not quite on board with the plan. He jumped in and out of boxes. At one point, he claimed a tattered sweater for himself by snatching a loose piece of yarn and running with it. Aria had no choice but to giggle as the handcrafted gift from her ex began unraveling. It had been the first time she laughed in the while.

"Thank you, Mr. Scissors. We need to have a bit more fun around here." Aria scooped him up and pressed her nose against his. The cat was no fool; he kept the yarn firmly clenched in his jaws.

Their cuddling session was interrupted by the doorbell. A quick look at her watch and Aria knew exactly who it was—Jehovah's Witnesses. They were the only ones up at 9am on a Saturday, hoping to catch people off guard. *Wait*, she thought, *I did see some Mormon missionaries in the neighborhood once.* Then, she envisioned a scenario where Witnesses and Mormons arrived at a house at the same time and started fighting over who got to claim the souls of the people inside.

The Witnesses were getting the upper hand, when the sound of Rachel's ringtone snapped Aria back to reality. Sighing, she answered the phone. They had spoken a few times since the incident, but the conversations were stilted and always drifted back to a topic Aria wanted to avoid. "Hey. I thought Saturday morning was your 'me' time. Shouldn't you be taking a hot bath or something?"

Rachel sounded tired. "Yeah. I'm going to watch a couple of DVDs and relax in a bit. What are you doing right now?"

"At this exact moment, I'm looking at junior prom dress and wondering why I thought burnt orange with hot pink was a sexy combination."

"So you are home. Jennifer is at your door; she wants to talk to you." When there was no response, Rachel sighed. "Please, Aria, this whole thing has been so hard for her."

"Hard for her? Really?"

"It's gotten around the office and co-workers are whispering behind her back. She is going to be haunted by this incident for the rest of her life. "

"What does any of that have to do with me?"

"If she can find a way to fix things with you, at least one piece of the burden would be lifted off of her."

Aria clenched her teeth to keep her tongue under control. It was as if the thread holding their friendship together had gotten even thinner. The Rachel she had met in college would have cut through Jennifer's bullshit with laser-like precision and dumped her months ago.

That was before they had been thrust into the real world and Rachel's mother started showing the first signs of Alzheimer's. Plus, Rachel had been nothing less than supportive when Aria had relationship dramas of her own.

The decision was made: Aria wasn't going to abandon her friend now. "No reason to avoid the inevitable. Tell her to give me a few minutes and

I'll let her in."

~

Five minutes later, Jennifer was standing in the living room, trying hard, Aria thought, to suppress a grin. "I'm sure Detective Fox has been in touch with you."

Aria nodded. "Maria's death was an accident. Her being in my house wasn't."

The sharp reply seemed to shock Jennifer and she cast her eyes downward. "I know you are angry and you have every right to be. I did something stupid, but you shouldn't take it out on Rachel. She's just being protective of me." Aria rolled her eyes. "Rachel misses you. If there is anything I can do to help us get past this—for her sake—let me know."

"I appreciate your concern, but Rachel and I are going to be fine. As far as you and I are concerned, we can't get past this unless you can explain the litter box."

Mr. Scissors hopped on the sofa. He feigned disinterest, but his ears stood at attention.

"Litter box?"

"Maria died Wednesday night. When I found her Friday, the food dish and water bowl were full— and the litter box was clean. This means that on more than one occasion, someone walked into my house and damn near stepped over the body."

Jennifer did not blink, but her voice cracked with uncertainty. "There's no legal obligation to report a death."

"What kind of coldhearted, psychopathic bitch would do that?"

Jennifer stared blankly at her for a few moments and then smiled. "I didn't know Maria that well. If she was as irresponsible as I was, anyone could have a key." Zipping up her jacket, she headed for the door. "I'd change the locks if I were you." The screen slammed shut behind her.

The loud noise caught Mr. Scissors by surprise but, otherwise, it had been an uneventful morning. He reached up the forbidden recliner and began scratching the handle.

"That's right, Mr. Scissors. It's time for the claws to come out."

.

The One Who Got Away

I just wanted to find a quiet corner to eat my veggie sticks—the only food on the buffet table that wouldn't upset my stomach. Before I could get a bite of celery, Myra had plopped down next to me.

"Star Trek was groundbreaking in tackling social issues," she began, "but what really interests me is how accurate the show was in regard to scientific theory."

I had been looking forward to the Baltimore B-Girls' Meet and Greet for weeks. Women who had been bickering and arguing online for years were finally going to see each other face to face. I wanted a front row seat to drama. Well, that's not what happened. It was a nice crowd, but the obnoxious assholes who started flame wars suddenly got shy. Instead of watching a live version of Jerry Springer, I ended up on the balcony with Myra.

"I don't mean that dilithium crystal bullshit, but intergalactic travel through wormholes." At this point, my brain started shutting down. Putting a picture of Mr. Spock on my profile had clearly been a mistake.

I was hungry and close to being bored to death when an angelic voice interrupted the lecture. "Myra, there's a car with its headlights on and someone said it was yours."

Myra jumped up, did the Vulcan hand gesture, and disappeared. I turned around to see who my savior was. The full, velvety voice belonged to the little twig of a woman who had kept to herself most of the night. "Hi, I'm picasogyrl627 aka Diana Davis." She extended her hand. "Myra means well, but she can be intense."

My fingers were fully engaged in carrot sticks by then, but I did manage a little wave. "Thank you, because I was not quite ready to be beamed up." After the first nibbles of food, my brain kicked back into action. I was in the presence of Dirty Diana.

About a year ago, a disgruntled ex-girlfriend sent an angry email meant for Diana to the entire list. It accused her of being possessive, obsessive, and just fucked up in general. There was a chorus of "she did it to me too" messages and her cover as a player was blown. To her credit, Diana did not allow herself to be baited into arguments. Her one message about the subject apologized to anyone who felt hurt but claimed that she wasn't prepared to address personal issues in a public forum.

I admit, I had wondered about the woman behind the controversy. She looked nothing like I expected. On the mailing list, she was always "my sister" this or "my people that." I just knew she was going to be pleasingly plump and wearing a dashiki. Okay, maybe not a dashiki, but I did expect kente cloth accessories.

Despite the heavy-looking rings on her right hand, Diana managed to flip a bit of weave over her shoulder. "I noticed you being selective in your food choices," she continued. "Are you a vegetarian or vegan?"

"Neither. I'm a steak and potatoes type of girl, but everything else out there was swimming in grease. Fat does not do a body good."

She stepped back and looked me over. "There's something incredibly sexy about a woman who takes care of herself."

I knew she was flirting and, if it were just her voice, I would have played into it. Diana wasn't sincere, though. Her eyes were vacant, like she had delivered that line a million times before. Ten minutes ago, she wouldn't have made eye contact with me, but suddenly I'm worthy? Princess Diana had decided to throw some of her precious attention my way because I was the best of a bad lot.

Yeah, I was getting agitated. So when she said, "I don't believe I got your name."

I responded, "That's because I didn't give it."

Diana tried to hide her shock behind a smile. "What do I call you?"

"The one who got away." I grabbed my plate and walked back into the party. I could feel her retinas trying to burn a hole through my back.

It was my turn to be surprised when, not twelve hours later, I got an email from picasogyrl627. The subject was "Hello, Chante." Diana had gotten my name and email address from Myra. Basically, she suggested I not believe rumor and innuendo. She just wanted to be friends. The last lines were cute. "I'm more resilient than the Borg Queen—so you know resistance is futile."

I felt sorry for Diana. How long did she have to listen to theories about the space-time continuum before Myra gave up my details? Besides, I hadn't dated anyone in forever and it felt nice to have someone interested.

However, I wasn't delusional about her motives either. Diana was only interested because I dissed her. I should have put a stop to it right then, but I didn't.

After all, I was curious, and Diana only wanted to be friends...

We exchanged numbers, but most of our conversations were via email. Her writing was funny, witty, and intelligent—no traces of the bored princess. We had private conversations about some of the topics that popped up on the B-Girls list—race, class, the death of our favorite club, where to buy quality sex toys, etc.

About a month into our friendship, we did stray into personal subjects, but Diana did not reveal much about her life. She had been out since puberty and was a part-time playwright—those were the only facts I could wrangle out of her.

Her favorite subject was me. What I liked, where I'd been. When I realized that she wasn't being forthcoming, I tried not to be so free about my own life. Though, I couldn't really blame her for being guarded—she had already been burnt by two or three women she had met online.

We began meeting up in person at the start of my accounting basics course. I had been thinking about taking a class for a while. Diana actually convinced me it was time to stop dreaming and start doing, The campus was near her place, so we'd meet in the courtyard after class to grab coffee. The first time she showed up, it was completely unexpected. She insisted on taking me to La Cafe Marchant to celebrate my return to academia. I rolled my eyes at that, but I'll never be one to turn down a free chocolate sundae.

It turned into a weekly ritual. Every Saturday, I left Professor Cho's ledgers and eased into Diana's Jeep. She tried to pay those other times too—but I insisted we go dutch. Now, she seemed like a different person. She listened attentively when I talked and I caught her admiring my assets on more than one occasion.

Gradually, Diana began mentioning her other email pen pals—and I didn't want to hear it. I didn't want to know about her and Myra comparing new theories of the space-time continuum or how Jackie—one of the main instigators of the witch-hunt—was being all apologetic now. One minute she was leaning in close and lightly stroking the back of my hand. The next, she was asking my advice on what to wear on a date. Can you believe I was jealous?

I tried to be cool about the situation, but I'm sure that my attitude got a little funky when she brought up the others. I can't explain it. My mind was creating a relationship that neither of us wanted. How did I start to think of her as mine?

These feelings freaked me out. I wanted to put a little distance between us, but how could I spend less time with Diana? It's not like we talked on the phone constantly or spent more than an hour together on the weekend.

At the end of a rough day, it was nice to read an uplifting message from her. And the days did get rough...

First off, I got a new roommate—courtesy of Craigslist. Out of the forty-two people who answered my ad, Khia seemed the most normal. She grew up in a rural town in Virginia with five older siblings and was finally striking out on her own. Living in Baltimore was going to be her grand adventure.

Unfortunately, she wanted me to be her new big sister and started treating my room like it was "our room." She used up my Peach Essence body wash like it was hers. I'd come home and it would be clear that someone had been lying in my bed, rifling through my old journals, etc. When I confronted her, she swore one of my sorority sisters came by or she had let one of my cousins in. A lie would come out of her mouth while she was wearing my stuff! So I was annoyed at home, which would have been easier to handle if I hadn't lost my job...

That's right. Some customer came in and complained to my manager on my day off. I didn't get a chance to hear what I was supposed to have done or mount any kind of defense. The front office had been looking for a reason to terminate me, so a situation that called for a written reprimand had me collecting my last check. The atmosphere at my job had been toxic for a while. I should have left instead of waiting for them to get rid of me.

Thankfully, I had enough money set aside to pay my expenses for a while. It was demoralizing. Here I am lecturing a twenty-three year old on being responsible and my thirty-two-year-old self couldn't handle my own business. Too embarrassed to tell anybody, every day I divided my time between disappointing interviews, bookstores, and cafes. I finally broke down when Diana noticed I had stopped complaining about work. I dissolved into a blubbering mess. It felt really good when she put her arm around my shoulder and dabbed my eyes.

After I got it all out, she took out her wallet. Before I could tell her that I didn't need money, she handed me a ticket. "The Baltimore Museum of Art is having a private showing of new acquisitions in the African Art collection. I know it's really short notice, but I thought you'd be interested."

"How did you get these!" Secretly, that had been my dream. To slip behind the scenes of a museum and peep at the art pieces that they keep behind closed doors. It's like being in a treasure trove. Hey, don't look at me like that—I did minor in art.

Diana's smile was wicked. "I have a friend who slips me a freebie from time to time. Meet you there at nine o'clock."

I was on time for once. After the opening remarks, the party broke down into various groups. This lot obviously knew each other and people gravitated to those they liked. I wanted to ask the curator a few questions, but Diana made sure we circulated throughout the crowd and spent a few minutes with each clique.

I felt a little awkward. I was the only woman there without a designer handbag. Diana was definitely in her element. I suspected that she was a patron who didn't need a mysterious friend to get an invitation.

By the end of the night, I was discussing the unsettling work of Kara Walker with a guy who had the worst toupee ever. During the whole exchange, he and Diana were grinning at each other like fools. He gave me his business card—it was the executive director—and asked me to call him about opportunities at the museum.

The next day, I sure did call him. After an explanation of what he was looking for, we agreed that I would make an excellent executive assistant. I almost choked on my mocha latte. It felt surreal until their human resource department called me up to officially offer the job.

Since I owed my good fortune to Diana, she was the first person I called to share the news. Of course, she already knew I would get the offer and invited me over for dinner to celebrate. That was when I found out she had a condo in Montgomery Cove. Either she was a well kept woman or she made more than enough for a BMA Patron membership.

I knew something was up the second she opened the door. For dinner with a friend, I had on my sneaks, jeans, and an over-sized t-shirt. Diana was in this jet-black, spaghetti-strapped slinky thingy and black stilettos. A sistah felt underdressed, okay? She whisked me in and sat me down in front of a plate of braised beef ribs, mac & cheese, and kale. Best of all, it was prepared the old-fashioned cholesterol-laden way my mother used to make it.

Between bites, I managed to ask, "How can you cook like this and stay that small?"

She tilted her head to the side and grinned slyly. "Tonight is all about you."

I helped her clear the table and that was when it really struck me how beautiful she was. It could have been the candlelight or the high of down-home comfort food, but her every move seemed graceful.

We moved over to the sofa and faux fireplace. Diana sat so close she almost ended up in my arms.

I wanted to kiss her so bad, but I caught myself before crossing that line. As I scooted over, she handed me a small gift-wrapped box from Jacques Torrez. They were my favorites—dark chocolate truffles infused with red wine.

Before I could take one, she swatted my hand away. "You've worked hard enough today," she said. Her manicure was raking my thigh and my nipples grew rock hard. Jeans be dammed, okay? After she put the first delicious morsel in my mouth, her fingers glided past my cheek and began lightly caressing my neck. She was just playing with my erogenous zones.

The first chocolate-drenched kiss was intoxicating. With my free hand, I cupped her ass and pulled her a little closer. The fingers working my thigh crept closer to my crotch. I tossed the box of candy aside and frantically tried to unbutton my fly. It was an unsuccessful attempt.

Lightly tugging my nipples, she led me to the bedroom. "I want to touch you in the soft places that you hide from everyone else." Bending me over the bed, Diana slid my jeans and thong to the floor. I tumbled forward, my ass sunny-side up. She flipped me over and her head disappeared under my shirt. As I was twisting my hips to meet her lips, I reached out for something to hold on to and found a blue nightshirt. I burrowed my face in it and smelled the essence of peaches. It had the same tear in the neckline and there were the faded dots where bleach had splashed on it.

My legs stiffened and my pussy pushed Diana out. "Chante, what's wrong?"

Sitting up, I hit the pillows and the missing pages from my journal flew into the air. I shoved Diana off of me and grabbed my clothes.

In the living room, I was hopping around like a crazy person trying to get dressed. Diana came out with a long scroll and calmly spread it across the coffee table. It was full of astrological graphs and symbols.

"I've done our charts," she said. "We are meant to be 'til death." Her voice was an eerie calm. "When I knew you were the one, I let the others go. We need each other."

I took note of the distance between her and the knife block. "No one needs you, Diana. I was doing just fine on my own."

"If it weren't for me, you would be still standing on your feet all day in that tired red smock directing people to housewares." Diana giggled to herself and took a sip of wine. "Your description of Williams' halitosis was on point."

The truth had finally started sinking in. Diana was the mysterious cousin who talked her way into my apartment and the irate customer who had complained to my manager.

It's hard to tie your shoes when your fingers are clenched into a fist, so I just stood up. "I'm going to leave now."

"Of course, you're angry—but it won't last. You'll be back. It's fate. You and I." Diana went to the door and opened it. Just as I was about to cross into freedom, she threw her arm in front of the exit. "You need me," she whispered. "More than that, you want me."

Anyone who saw me walking back to my car must have thought I was crazy. How could I let myself think that any part of Diana was sincere? The meal flip-flopped in my stomach. Was this some Hannibal Lecter shit?

I was too paranoid to go home. Did she bug my

room? Did she have her own key to my place? Who knew what other areas of my life she had violated. I drove all the way to DC and checked into a Motel 6. Within minutes, the shower was on full blast. I wanted to scrub everything away.

I was disgusted with myself. What was I going to do? Drop out of class? Turn down the job offer?

The worst part was that she was right. Through my anger, pain, and frustration, part of me still wanted her. I thought about what the night would have been like if I hadn't grabbed the shirt.

I'm sure Diana put it there on purpose, though. She wanted me to find it—to show me that she was really in control. Part of me wanted to submit, just let her have her way. I took the handheld showerhead and let the water gently massage my clit. The release was breathtaking.

Stepping out of the bathroom was like stepping back into common sense. The insane desire for Diana had passed. Toweling off, I heard my cell phone buzzing away. She had sent a text: *You belong to me. 'Til death do us part.*

I laughed. *No, baby*, I thought. *You picked the wrong one this time.*

Then, there was a knock on the door...

Witness

Tracking down the country home of reclusive actress Monica Little hadn t been easy, but Longworth wanted the money shot. As darkness settled over the isolated estate, he crept along the bushes with his lens trained on the back of the house.

Waiting for the star to appear, Longworth was startled by a gunshot. Henri, Monica's latest lover, emerged from the woods dragging a sack behind him. He stopped next to a freshly dug hole—a grave—and fell to his knees.

The bag stirred.

Fueled by terror, the paparazzo rushed Henri from the side and smashed his camera into the Frenchman's jaw. Reaching for the bag, Longworth felt warmth...flesh and bone. Tearing apart the plastic, he found—a deer.

Henri struggled to his feet. "Idiot," he hissed through a bloody mouth. "I don't bury her! I dig her up!"

The rejuvenated woman ascended from her

retreat. Loose bits of earth fell from her brown, ethereal frame as she bathed in moonlight. The smile she graced Henri with turned vicious when her gaze fell upon the interloper. A tongue flickered over jagged teeth.

Monica Little was hungry.

Losing Michelle

Maura swerved to avoid the tree that suddenly appeared in the headlights. The car veered off the narrow road and landed in a ditch. The impact triggered the airbags and the force of their deployment shattered all of the windows. Catching her breath, Shana forced her way out of the car and staggered through mud and glass to the driver's side door. She pulled a semi-conscious Maura out and both of them leaned against the side of the Volkswagen. "Come on, baby," Shana said, "snap out of it. We can't stop now."

Maura took a step and thought her legs would give way. Grabbing on to the broken window to steady herself, she felt the remaining shards slicing through her fingers. "I can't," she whimpered. "What are those things? Why is this happening to us?"

Shana pulled Maura into her arms and held her tight. They stood for a few moments in the dark silence, clinging to each other desperately.

Then, a low rumbling sounded in the distance. Maura turned to look down the road and saw their pursuers—an army of the undead—shambling toward them. She reached inside the car to turn off the headlights, but it was too late. "They know we're here!"

Shana pointed to a house at the top of a hill. "We'll take cover there. Go!" Maura nodded and took off running. Shana grabbed the shotguns from the backseat and followed her.

It wasn't until they had forced through the back door of the building that they realized they had run into a funeral home.

~

Evelyn Foster spent the next fifteen minutes staring as her pen stood motionless against the page. She had no idea what should happen next and ripped the stillborn idea to shreds. It was the third time that morning her imagination had stalled.

None of the usual creativity engines helped. Writing exercises were a waste of time. She felt detached from the words—her own words. Closing her laptop and switching to paper hadn't worked. It doesn't matter what medium is used to record the story if there is no story to tell.

Her growling stomach gave Eve an excuse to leave her barren, windowless cubbyhole. She opened the door and was immediately greeted by the scent of Michelle's apple turnovers. Maybe food was the answer. The condo was so small that it only took five steps to put her at the kitchen table. What it was lacking in size it made up for in the view—ceiling-to-floor windows overlooking the bay.

"How's it going?" Michelle asked as she pulled a tray of apple turnovers out of the oven.

"It's not." Eve hugged her girl from behind, reached around her ample bosom for a treat, and got a hand smack for her troubles. "Aww, come on. I'm suffering over here."

"These are for little Nate's bake sale. Big Nate was supposed to make chocolate chip cookies, but he let them burn up while he was playing the Wii."

Eve shook her head. "And Michelle saves the day." She and Michelle had been together off and on throughout college but went their separate ways after graduation. When they kept finding themselves in the same social circles, they thought maybe they should try the relationship again as adults. It seemed like they made the right choice—

most days.

"I was about to call you for lunch anyway." The cook put a layer of fresh mozzarella over last night's lasagna and put it in the still hot oven. "Do you think it's writer's block?"

Eve poured herself some iced tea and sat at the table. "I get the seed of an idea, but just when I think I have a handle on the plot, it slips away."

"That little airless room is a walk-in closet. You should at least try working in the living room."

She knew Michelle was trying to help, but Eve felt herself getting defensive. "No, I need a place to concentrate. No internet, no television, no birdies chirping at the window—"

"And no ideas flowing through. You didn't need total silence and peace when you were writing *The Bite of the Ballanger*."

Eve smiled. She had written the book about humans caught in a war between zombies and vampires between classes. It wasn't supposed to be a real novel at all, just a procrastination project that filled the time she should have been studying. The novel and its sequel did end up getting published, but they quickly went out of print. She had moved on, gotten a life and a real job.

Now, six years later, urban fantasies featuring female heroes were popular. To keep up with the current trend, her publisher slapped a new cover on *The Bite of the Ballanger*—the sexiest dead women you'd ever want to meet—and it was an instant success. Her literary agent tracked her down to deliver a sizeable royalty check and an offer for two more sequels.

"That was before there was any money on the line." Eve had originally thought of the new book deal as a way to pay off her student loans. Now she owed words, not money.

"But it's just a story, right? The manuscript for the novel isn't due for another five months."

"It's a contribution to 'The Year's Best Dark Fantasy & Horror' and the deadline is next Tuesday. If I can't scratch out a decent story, I might as well forget about writing anything else."

The timer went off and Michelle went to check on the food. She kissed Eve on the forehead. "Maybe if you relax a little bit, it will give one of those seeds time to flower. Cocktails with Gina and

Shanice will be right on time."

"Is that tonight?" Eve winced. "Baby, I'm not going to be able to make it. I'm not leaving the house until I get something decent down on paper."

"You do plan on accompanying me to this, right?" Michelle handed her a flier for the Black Pride fundraiser. "It's a dinner cruise around the harbor. I'm on the committee; what's it going to look like if I'm there without you?"

"Baby, I'm sorry. I forgot about this."

"You seem to forget about anything that includes me." Michelle took the warmed lasagna out of the oven. "Your deadline is in seven days. The cruise is in three. It's one evening..."

"I can't make you any promises." The writer shrugged.

"You don't want to go out anymore. You don't want to do anything."

"But I'm not stopping you from going out. Why don't you disappear for a while?" Eve sucked her teeth and the facade of domestic bliss was broken. "You didn't used to be so goddamned codependent."

"What's wrong with you?" Michelle sounded exasperated. "What's wrong with us?"

"Nothing is wrong with me. I'm just trying to get this work done."

"That lie would be easier to swallow if you were actually writing." Michelle took off her apron, folded it neatly, and dropped it in Eve's lap. "You can serve yourself."

After gathering the fragments from the trash, Eve spent the next few hours trying to rework the stories she had started. None of them felt right. The balance with her main characters was off, like the balance in her own life. She hadn't forgotten about the cruise, but she lied to upset Michelle. Picking a fight—a bullshit one at that—was a form of procrastination.

With the right prodding, Michelle could scream, cry, and go into a full-scale production. At least, that was how it used to be. Now, she clammed up and left the room. Eve wondered if she had pushed too far and the dynamics of their relationship were changing. It had spilled over into her work; the characters weren't talking to her either.

The first time Michelle called, she ignored the phone. The second time, Eve ignored it and switched the phone to "silent" mode. She felt it was too soon to give in and she didn't want to admit that she hadn't made any progress.

Eve looked up at the ceiling and sighed. Trying to convert the closet to an office was a bad idea. She decided to set up camp in the living room. Passing the kitchen, she saw an apple turnover left on the stove. The pastry was a warning. She hadn't pushed too far, but she had to reverse course. Michelle had left without saying goodbye.

After settling in her favorite chair, a plush recliner facing that fantastic view of the bay, Eve fell asleep.

Moonlight and hunger stirred her awake. "Michelle?" She grabbed her phone. It was 7:38. She pushed herself out of the chair and looked around the darkened room. Michelle hadn't come back at all. She drew the curtains and turned on the lights. There weren't any more missed calls, but the bank had sent her an email alert: the balance for their joint account had dipped below $10,000.

Eve was shocked—neither of them touched the money without talking to the other first. For the account to be that low, Michelle had to withdraw over $5000.

If this was a new way of getting her attention, it had worked. Eve called Michelle and was ready to start round two. "What's up?" a deep, masculine voice answered. Eve's tongue was paralyzed. She heard another man in the background. "We need to get rid of this bitch! Drop her right off the face of the motherfucking Earth."

The call disconnected.

Officer Juanita Childress took off her shoes and flexed her tired feet. The only thing stopping her from stripping down completely and enjoying a eucalyptus bubble bath was the anxious woman wearing another groove in her tattered carpet. Sighing, Childress settled for the temporary comfort of a self-administered foot message. "Michelle isn't missing. Didn't you pick another fight with her?"

"What does that have to do with anything?" Eve could barely sit still. She knew a person needed to be gone at least twenty-four hours before the police would even take a missing person's report, so she had contacted to a friend on the force.

"Maybe she finally decided to leave your ass, took her share of the money, and skipped off with her boyfriend."

Eve's cheeks flushed in anger. "She doesn't have a boyfriend."

Standing to stretch, Childress felt her knee pop. "That's how it was in college. Y'all would fight and she would run right back to her ex-boyfriend."

"Yeah, and I would run to you." Eve rolled her eyes. "That's all in the past."

"Are you sure? She's gone and look where you are."

"I'm here for your badge. Can you start thinking like a cop and not a psycho ex-girlfriend?"

"I am thinking like a cop. I don't want to go on some stupid search with you just to find out that she's with a lover or over her mother's house."

"The men on the phone called Michelle a bitch and talked about getting rid of her." Officer Childress rolled her eyes, but Eve was adamant. "I didn't dial a wrong number. She's in trouble. It may already be too late."

The cop put her shoes back on. "If this winds up being some lovers' quarrel shit, you owe me a full spa day. Come on, we'll take my car."

Once they were both strapped in, Officer Childress pointed to the glove department. "Grab a tissue, clean yourself up, and then center yourself." She started the Jeep and headed south. "First we'll drive down to the precinct to check on reports of women in hospitals or hurt, etc. If there's no match, we'll try to retrace her movements."

Eve nodded. "Thanks, Juanita. I know Michelle isn't exactly your favorite person."

"I protect and serve all people." At a stop light, Officer Childress stared down a group of teens on the corner who hastily thrust their hands in their pockets and dispersed. "What was Michelle's schedule like? Why are you just missing her now?"

Eve stared back at her blankly. "I don't know. She made cookies for her nephew. They needed to be delivered by noon. She was supposed go to Gina's place for cocktails at eight. I was supposed to go too, but I backed out."

"Backed out? I like seeing Gina every chance I get. What about the time in between? You didn't expect her to come back home?"

"I just assumed she went shopping or something. She called me twice, but I didn't answer."

"Damn." Officer Childress rolled her eyes.

"I feel bad enough about it, okay? I was working. How could I know something was wrong?"

"Okay, so Gina hasn't seen her either?"

"I don't know."

The cop pulled into the parking lot of a 7-11 and rested her head against the steering wheel. "I don't believe this shit. You never called Gina?"

"With the missing money and the guy's voice, I just thought—"

"Don't you think Gina would have called to see what was happening if both of you decided not to show up?" Promising herself at least five hours of uninterrupted sleep, Childress turned the car around. "Michelle and Gina are probably knocking back martinis and talking about your trifling ass. I'm taking you to your girl and I still want my spa day!"

Though they drove the rest of the way in silence, Eve was relieved. She had gone into panic mode and lost her common sense. It was probably just a joke. She had ignored Michelle, so her girl had taken it a step further and handed the phone to someone else.

Once on Gina's porch, they heard muffled music coming from behind the front door. Eve felt herself getting angry. "I'm gonna be pissed if Michelle is in there."

The cop laughed. "Well, that's one way to get you out of the house."

The door swung open and Gina appeared with a drink in one hand and a phone clasped to her ear. She motioned for them to come in.

There was no party. The music and laughter were coming from the television. "I'll call you back later," Gina told the person on the other end of the line. She kissed Officer Childress on the cheek and gave Eve an air kiss. "It's nice to see that you changed your mind." She looked around behind both of them. "Where's Michelle?"

Eve's heart sank. "She's not here?"

"I haven't seen her since she left for the bank."

"Fuck," Officer Childress whispered. Eve crossed her arms and closed her eyes.

Gina looked from one to the other and then turned off the television. "What's going on?"

Eve blinked back tears. "I don't know where she is."

Gina turned to Childress. "Tell me she's not serious."

"Gina, this is very important," Childress said firmly. "Tell us what happened this afternoon."

Understanding the gravity of the situation, Gina sat her pleasingly plump frame on the arm of the sofa. "Michelle came over earlier and we went shopping." She turned to Eve. "She was pissed at you and wanted to do a little retail therapy. While we were out, she got a phone call from the Starlight Cruise business manager. The Black Pride fundraising committee had given him a check that bounced. If he didn't get the last payment in cash by this evening, the boat wouldn't be leaving the dock. Michelle said she would make sure the boat was secure and then find out what the hell happened."

"Do you know how much money she needed?" Childress asked.

"About $5700."

Eve couldn't believe what she was hearing. "She was carrying over $5000 and you let Michelle go to some damn dock by herself?"

"She wasn't supposed to be going alone," Gina said. "She wanted you to meet her at the bank. Didn't she call you?"

Eve was stunned into silence.

"None of that matters right now," Officer Childress said. "Where did you have this conversation about the dock and the bank?"

"We were in the food court."

The cop shook her head. "So anyone within earshot could have heard Michelle say that she was going to withdraw a large sum from the bank. About what time did you and Michele part ways?"

"4:30."

"Okay. The last call Eve received from her was at 5:15. We're about three hours behind."

~

Back in the Jeep, Childress stayed in professional mode. "We're going to keep following her trail for now. If we stop to file a report, they still won't look for her. A man's voice and missing money isn't enough to accelerate an investigation."

Eve dialed Michelle again and, like the other hundred times, it rang once and switched over to voicemail. "Hold on, baby. We're coming."

The marina was not the abandoned wasteland that Eve had imagined it to be, but the building that housed the Starlight Cruises office was dark. "What are we going to do now?"

"Follow me." Childress got out of the car and approached the guardhouse.

"This place is closed. What are you doing?" Eve envisioned her girlfriend at the bottom of a ditch with the life slowly leaching out of her. "We're wasting time."

Childress knocked on the little plywood shack and an elderly guard appeared at the window. The plastic tag pinned to his loose shirt had "Pearce" typed on it. "Are you the ladies who were supposed to meet Mr. Riley? He left hours ago."

Eve left the two of them at the gate and sat on a concrete bench along the pier. Every scene of debauched violence she had ever penned came back to taunt her—with Michelle as the victim.

Why did she create horror stories when the world had so many real ones? How many unspeakable acts were occurring under those beautiful, cold lights?

To take someone off the face of the Earth, you put them under. Under dirt, under water. She looked at the black waves rolling ashore and wondered.

A hand clasped her shoulder. "Come on. We've got work to do."

Eve shrugged Childress off. "It's too late."

"No, we don't have time for this pity party shit. If money is the target, then they will want to empty the account. They will need Michelle alive to make another face-to-face withdrawal."

"What if money wasn't the target?"

The cop shook her head. "Going that route doesn't do anyone any good. Michelle just happens to disappear when she's got a wad of cash on her? I don't believe in coincidence." Childress flipped through her notebook and circled a word. "Who else is on this committee? She probably called one of them and it's a good chance that one of them is a thief."

Combing her memory, Eve struggled to come up with the names. "Michelle has been talking about this for weeks, but I haven't really been listening. I'm sure it's all on her computer."

"The next stop is your place."

Her battery low, Eve wanted to throw her phone out of the window. If they were in a police car, there would be a siren and traffic would part for them. "I don't understand. Why isn't what we know now enough to file a report?"

"You asked for my help, so trust that I know what I'm doing."

"It's not like you're a detective or anything." Eve regretted it the moment the words slipped off of her tongue. "I didn't mean that."

"Yes, you did. I've been cussed out and had my intelligence questioned by more people than you know. You're scared, I understand." Childress hit her brakes. "Isn't that Michelle's car?"

Michelle's little Volkswagen was neatly tucked away in its assigned parking space. Eve looked up at their condo and the lights were on. "She's home!"

Childress had to stop Eve from jumping out of the car. "Whoa. We're going up together."

After the attendant at the front desk confirmed that Michelle had returned alone, both Eve and Childress were visibly relieved. The officer looked at her watch. "You got me so worked up, I'll be lucky if I get a nap before I go back on duty."

Eve gave her a quick hug and stepped into the elevator. "Thank you so much."

"You still owe me that spa day," Childress called through the closing doors.

Her hands shaking, Eve barely got the key in the lock before Michelle opened the door. She was in her nightshirt and fuzzy slippers. "You can't go out with me, but you have time to hang out with your ex?"

Ignoring the jab, Eve threw her arms around her girlfriend and covered her face with kisses. "Baby, we've been all over this city looking for you."

Michelle laughed. "I know. I called Gina to give her the scoop on what happened and she told me that you had shown up with Juanita."

"What happened?"

"When I couldn't reach you, I asked Riley, the manager, to meet me at the bank. After I settled with him, I met with the rest of the committee and we decided to confront Narcia, the treasurer, directly. She told some sob story about falling behind in her car payments."

"What's going to happen to her?"

"Well, I made it very clear to her that she owes us and not Black Pride. On the way home, Fantasia started screaming from my purse. That's when I realized Jeffery and I switched phones. It took me another hour to track him down to get my phone back."

Take that bitch off the face of the Earth. The clouds parted from Eve's mind. They were talking about Narcia.

"I stopped to pick up some ribs from Shorty's and here I am." At the mention of food, Eve's stomach suddenly remembered that it hadn't eaten in hours. Michelle recognized the look of desperate hunger. "Of course I got an order for you too." She took a greasy white bag out of the refrigerator.

After dinner, Eve went to the window and looked across the bay at the dock where she feared the worst. "When I couldn t find you, it was as if the whole world was gone. Promise you won't disappear on me like that again."

"Let's get one thing clear," Michelle said, her eyes cold and dark. "If one of us ever disappears, it's going to be you."

In Remembrance of Her

The smell of fresh cut grass lingered in the autumn breeze. Laura zipped up her jacket. The trees shielding Bellcreek Plantation from the main road also cast a permanent shadow on the grounds. Even the tombstones seemed to absorb rather than reflect the rays of the sun. Looking out into the woods, Laura felt unseen eyes were returning her gaze. She couldn't believe that Nia was here, secreted away from the realm of the living.

Hearing the rustling of brittle leaves under foot, Laura turned to find Paul stalking toward her. An older man with graying temples, he had never tried to conceal his hatred. "You don't belong here," Nia's brother began. "All we have is her memory and you coming around only rubs salt in the wound."

Behind him, she saw the other siblings and cousins on the porch—the close-knit family Nia had abandoned to make a life with her. "It's not fair for you to keep her from me. I lost her too. I lost everything."

"You're trespassing."

"All she talked about was the family, this land, the history of this place. How the family was able to hold on to the acreage through generations. She didn't leave. You pushed her away."

Paul closed his eyes and took a slow, deep breath. "My sister loved you. That's the only reason we haven't called the police. There's nothing for you here. You're trespassing."

Laura watched him walk back to Bellcreek Manor. The others had already gone inside, but she knew they were staring at her through the delicate lace curtains.

~

She got a queasy feeling in front of Cafe Diana, but Laura forced herself to go inside. It was the same liberal arts college crowd, mostly female and white. She picked a bear claw from the assortment of goods under the glass case and shocked the waitress when she paid with cash. Taking a window seat, she had a clear view of the park.

It had been a year since the assassination. The media would call it a random act of violence, but Laura knew there was nothing random about it. They had just left Cafe Diana—it had been her idea to end the evening with a moonlit stroll—when someone fired three shots into Nia's back. There had been screams, running, and madness. She would never forget the look of shock on her lover's face or her convulsions in the grass.

Community leaders suggested, as tastefully as possible, that some unsavory element had followed Nia to their academic enclave. Then, a witness came forward with a description of the shooter—a white, middle-aged male wearing dark clothes who escaped in a waiting truck. The next day, editorials in the college paper lamented over whether or not their humble little area had a "race" problem. Everyone wanted to forget the actual murder as soon as possible.

Laura wished she could cry, but too many tears had been shed already. "Excuse me, is this seat taken?" The question came from a guy wearing sweats.

"No," she said, expecting him to take the chair and join the group next to her. Instead, he took up half the space on her table with his backpack.

"Hi, I'm Jeffrey." He extended his hand, a silver ring depicting a crucified Christ nearly blinding her. He retracted it awkwardly when she didn't return the greeting.

Laura got up and tossed the uneaten pastry in the trash. She could hear him protesting and apologizing, but the words sounded unclear, distant.

The sun had disappeared and warm amber hues had spread across the cloudless sky. Laura walked across the street and toward the place she last held her lover's hand. The park was full of students and people letting their dogs or children roam free. They acted as if they were in a bubble of protection and immune to violence. Laura could never feel safe or loved or whole again.

Someone grabbed her arm and she wheeled around, ready to fight. Jeffrey saw her defensive stance and took a step back. "Whoa! Is this book yours? You left it on the floor."

"No, it's not mine." Seeing his face against the backdrop of the trees triggered a memory. Suddenly, Laura recognized him as one of the people who had actually come over to help. "I'm sorry, you look familiar."

He nodded, relieved. "I know this is awkward, but I just wanted to know if everything was all right. Did they ever find out who did it?" They began walking toward the fountain in the middle of the square.

Laura shook her head. "It will be a year tomorrow and I still have no idea who or why. I want to thank you for doing what you could to make her final moments…" Her voice trailed off.

A cold wind swirled the leaves and the moon faded into view. Laura threw two pennies into the fountain and they sat on a bench. "We were going to stop here to make a wish."

Jeffrey's unzipped his backpack. "I have some information about that night." His hands shook as they retrieved a binder. "I think I can give you some answers."

It was Laura's turn to grab him. "You know who did this?"

"She had to be stopped," said a gruff voice from behind. Laura whirled around to find a pair of ragged old men who looked like they had just pulled themselves out of the grave. It was the one with the exquisitely carved cane that spoke. "She was evil. The whole lot of them prey on us like sheep. Tell her, Phil."

His companion, Phil, nodded. "Wolf and man cannot abide together. They hunt us for sport."

Laura could barely control her anger. "This is a sick joke."

"It's not a joke," Jeffrey assured her.

Agitated, the old guy took a small dagger out of his belt. "How do we know she's not one of them? You can't live with them and not be tainted."

Jeffrey nodded. "She wouldn't touch my ring."

Laura stepped back until her calves hit the side of the fountain. She looked around frantically for a crowd to run to, but everyone else had retreated to the outskirts of the park.

A policeman stepped from around the hedges. "The park is closing, folks." He looked at the gleaming blade. "Hey, what's going on over here?"

Laura ran to his side. "Those people are crazy. They are talking about wolves and evil. That one tried to stab me."

The cop sighed. "Hold out your hand, Miss." He put a silver bullet in her palm and closed her fingers around it.

"What the hell are you doing?" she asked.

The policeman winked and shushed her. When it was obvious that she wasn't being tormented by the metal, he let her go. "Are you satisfied, Patch? The woman is just as human as you are, maybe more so."

Patch put the weapon back in its holster and used Phil's shoulder to right himself. "Sorry, Officer Danvers. Can't be too careful."

Officer Danvers took back the bullet and motioned to the park entrance. "Let me walk you to your car." They started back down the cobblestone path. "I'm sorry about that. Patch is a good man, but his world is a little warped." After a few moments of silence, he cleared his throat. "He's right about the wolves, though. It sounds incredible, but I know it's true. I've seen their victims."

Laura wondered if she inadvertently stepped into the *Twilight Zone*. "You're admitting to me that you killed her," she yelled. "Is that what you want me to believe? She was shot because she was a werewolf?"

A couple walking in the opposite direction stared

at them.

Danvers tugged her arm. "You don't really want to do that. A belligerent, unstable woman roaming around the park can easily find herself confined to the psycho ward of Marsden Medical for observation."

She snatched away from him. "Is that a threat?"

"All I ask is that you hear us out. Our society, an international organization, has had Nia and her ilk under surveillance for a long time. When she met you, she tried to tame the beast within and failed. They can only live as human for so long before the bloodlust overtakes them." Danvers took off his hat and wiped his brow with his forearm. "After months of inactivity, Nia would go into a feeding frenzy. After she had her fill of flesh, she moved on. That's why you never stayed in the same city for more than two years."

Jeffrey reappeared at her side and thrust the binder into her arms. "The evidence is here; look at it. We aren't crazy and we don't kill for pleasure." His eyes had lost their soft, boyish charm. "Your bitch was deadly."

Murder in the city is random and inevitable. Millions of people crammed into close quarters, breeding anger, hatred, and despair—it was an atmosphere that stoked the dark side of human nature. This had always been Laura's philosophy, so she had never paid much attention to the news.

Now, in her hotel room with the "evidence" spread out before her, she began to reconsider that theory. Articles described mangled bodies and speculation that wolves or voodoo practitioners were at fault. Crime scene photos displayed slashed throats and ripped flesh. She created a timeline and mapped it against the murders. Danvers was right, there did seem to be a pattern.

Then, there was the incident. Ten months after they initially moved in together, their relationship was rapidly deteriorating. Nia had become cold and Laura didn't know how to reach her. Then, Laura came home one night and found a trail of tattered, bloody clothing that stretched from the living room to the bathroom.

Nia was in the shower, a pool of pink water at her feet. She said that she'd been in a car accident. Laura had wanted to take her to the hospital, but there was so much urgency and passion in Nia's kisses... They reconnected as lovers that night.

Between caresses and gentle bites, Laura had found a scratch here and there, but all that blood had to have come from someone else.

Laura's gaze drifted back to a photograph of a young woman whose face had been torn away. She began to cry.

After checking out, Laura noticed Phil waiting for her in the lobby. She took the binder out of her duffle bag. "Take this and leave me alone."

"Where are you going?"

"Home." She began walking the long corridor towards the parking lot. "There really is nothing left for me here."

The old man nearly broke out in a trot to keep up with her pace. "We need your help."

"You've got to be kidding. First, you took her away from me. Then, you tell me that the best years of my life were a fucking illusion."

Phil managed to block her path. "No one does this because they want to. We are conscripted into service when the evil touches our lives." He took out the picture of a young man with an exposed ribcage. "This was Peter, my son. When it intrudes on your world, there are only two responses: fear or love. Fear is a flight from the truth, but you can't outrun it. It's always with you. I fight them now out of love for my boy."

It's true, Laura thought. *I'll never be able to forget…* "What do you need me to do?"

With a sad, understanding smile, Phil took her hand and led her to a waiting town car. Behind the wheel, Danvers was out of uniform and Jeffrey rode shotgun. Laura found herself between Phil and a stranger in an expensive suit. "Bill, boys, meet our new recruit."

Danvers nodded to her before merging onto the expressway. "Welcome aboard."

Laura turned to Phil. "I asked what you wanted, but I haven't agreed to do anything." Her anxiety grew as the city disappeared behind them.

Phil continued, "Attacks in our area have ramped up since…since Nia. We thought she was rogue. We didn't know the pack was so close."

"You've already helped a great deal," Danvers said. "We found the pack by following you to their estate. Now we need you to help us get inside."

Laura shook her head. "No, no way. I'm not going back up there."

"It's a reconnaissance mission." Phil put a hand on her knee. "We've had the property under surveillance, but Bill needs to scout out the plantation itself. Only one is there now, the man with the graying temples."

"That's Paul," she said, "and he's not going to let me in."

Bill opened up his briefcase. "I'm sure he will when you show him this." Carefully, unfolding a handkerchief, he presented her with a ruby and gold ring. Nia's ring.

If Laura's eyes were lasers, they would have bored a hole into the back of Jeffrey's skull. "You stripped that right off of her finger."

"Jeffrey took this as a trophy for me," Bill boasted. "I'm the one who shot her."

Sensing her rising anger, Phil whispered in her ear, "Forget the woman that you loved and remember the monster that she was. Remember the monster."

~

Danvers, Jeffrey, and Phil got out of the car at the beginning of the winding road that led to Bellcreek Plantation. Bill had taken over the driving and Laura was silent. "I'm your lawyer," he said. "You are returning the ring on one condition: they agree not to press charges. I've got a release for them to sign."

"And then?" Laura asked.

"Then, we wing it."

The dismal plantation house came into view. Sunlight illuminated the cracked paint and splintering wood. A knot of dread gurgled in Laura's stomach. "Phil said that his kid was killed. Why do you do this?"

Bill parked on the gravel driveway. "Survival of the fittest. Phil tries to be all philosophical about it, but humans are animals too."

When Paul opened the door, Laura played her part. "I have something you want." She showed him the ring.

His jaw stiffened, but Paul led them into the office. "Give it to me," he said.

Bill took a document from his briefcase. "We are prepared to return the property, if you agree not to penalize my client for misplacing it."

His ear twitching, Paul ignored Bill and held out his hand. Laura gave him the ring to examine. "My lawyer has been holding on to it. It was kept out of spite. I'm sorry."

Paul's smile was unsettling. "No, I'm sorry. For what it's worth, Nia was right about you." He walked around to a well-stocked mini-bar. "As always, I've been rude. Would either of you like a drink?" Rather than wait for an answer, he picked up a decanter of port and brought it down hard on Bill's head.

The commotion drew another man, an obvious relative, into the room. "There are three more at the bottom of the hill," he said. "The two older men we saw yesterday and a boy."

"They claimed to be part of a secret society," Laura said.

Paul's laugh was frightening. "The whelp will be

easy to break; he'll lead us to the others." The men lifted Bill to his feet and stripped him of his weapons. Paul gave her back the ring. "We are going to meet his friends. You take him."

Laura grabbed Bill by the back of his coat and dragged him up the stairs. She opened the door to the master bedroom and pulled him inside. The huddled mass in the bed stirred. "Nia, this is the one. This is the coward that violated you." The lump of flesh uncoiled into a woman. Her eyes — feral.

Bill shook like a rabbit. "It can't be!"

When the cracked lips peeled back to reveal a muzzle, Laura turned away. She didn't want to see the change. Screams were replaced by the sound of claw against wood and snapping bones.

After what seemed like an eternity, hairy hands with extended fingers gently pulled Laura into an embrace. The ring was back in its rightful place. Nia would be whole again.

Laura had chosen love and its path of darkness.

Should Have Seen It Coming

Val ate carefully over a napkin to keep pizza crumbs from staining the contracts on her desk. Usually, she met friends for lunch at Luisa's Cantina, but a recent acquisition by her company put an end to that. The Petrovski/Rossi Group had bought sassy-but-struggling startup Iconic Enterprises to "strengthen its presence in the emerging digital media market." The legal scrutiny was over and investors had blessed the deal. Now came the hard work of amending contracts and reassuring Iconic's clients.

Iconic employees? Some would get absorbed into P & R; most would get a pink slip. Thankfully, Val had nothing to do with Human Resources and would not be involved with the great purge.

Three years ago, it was Val's job on the line. Petrovski merged with Rossi and the new regime quickly began letting people go. Senior officials were given parties and packages. Lower level employees simply vanished.

Suddenly, the accolades and commendations Val earned in the past meant nothing. She had to impress a new boss who treated her like a new hire.

Being one of a handful of black people in her division, Val always felt the pressure to perform. The merger pushed her workaholic tendencies into overdrive. She absorbed the work of her peers who were let go and volunteered for projects. It meant more meetings, more headaches, and more time spent away from home.

The next pepperoni-drenched bite tasted good going in but touched off a bout of indigestion. Val threw the slice back in the box and shoved it aside. The cry of a frustrated baby erupted from her cell phone. She rolled her eyes and swiveled around to the large window that gave her a panoramic view of skyscrapers.

Professionally, working long hours had paid off. Val had earned a promotion and an assistant to handle mundane tasks.

Unfortunately, it also led to the end of her four-year relationship with Gloria. The two were nearly inseparable in the beginning. After the merger, Val had less and less time for weekend adventures. In an attempt to make it work, they swapped their separate apartments for a shared townhouse.

If Gloria didn't like spending weekends at home, she absolutely hated eating alone - after making meals for two. The daughter of a former pro-football player who became a multimillionaire by investing wisely, she didn't understand Val's economic anxiety. The family fortune allowed Gloria to approach life fearlessly.

Lose one job? You'll get another. Business go under? Take the tax write-off and start another venture. Why worry about supporting yourself, when your girlfriend's parents love and treat you like part of the family?

Gloria began playfully referring to herself as a corporate widow and Val reluctantly acknowledged the tension in their relationship. When a stranger at the party admonished Val for neglecting "a sexy little mami like Gloria," that was a five-alarm sign of trouble. Val hoped two weeks in the Bahamas would fix everything. She never got a chance to buy the tickets.

The breakup was abrupt.

Val came home to a quiet house. She was happy about it at first. She thought Gloria had gone to bed or gone out. It would be a rare evening of no arguments. Forty-five minutes later, she realized that Gloria's clothes and shoes were gone.

For days, tearful calls to Gloria went to voicemail. When she did answer, it was to drive her message home. "You only paid attention to me when you were on the verge of losing me," Gloria said. "You gave me enough to feel optimistic, to convince me to hang around for a while longer. Then you ignore me again. You aren't going to change. It has to be me." It wasn't an argument or a point to be debated. Gloria hung up and calls went back to voicemail again.

That was why now, when Gloria's ringtone - the crying baby - filled the office, Val didn't bother to look at her phone. The ex had been calling and texting all morning. To be so desperately wanted after being discarded and dismissed? Revenge was more than sweet; it was delicious.

Play time was over. Val turned off the cell phone and pulled the pile of contracts back towards her.

Totally emerged in work, she reflexively answered her office phone when it rang. "Petrovski / Rossi International, Valerie Dawson speaking. How may I help you?"

"Valerie, please listen to me."

Gloria's voice caught Val by surprise. *Two points for you*, she thought. Val took a deep breath and tried to keep the atmosphere professional. "I'm surprised to hear from you, Ms. Crandle. You made it clear in our last conversation that you no longer required my services."

"Val, there are some things I need to get from the house. They are in a box; I think I left it beside the sofa."

"Ms. Crandle, didn't you plan your exit accordingly?"

"Don't do this."

Val smirked. "Do what? In any case, if you've tried to get back into the home, you've discovered that I now lock the storm door." Gloria never got around to making a duplicate set of keys for herself. "I've also changed the codes on the security alarm. As a woman living alone, I take my security seriously."

Gloria's hesitant response meant she was trying to keep her own anger under control. "These are pictures, cards, family memories - personal items that don't mean a thing to you."

"Couldn't have meant that much; you left it behind."

"Just put it out on the porch. I can pick it up and be on my way."

"If I touch that box, it's going in the trash. You can pick your damn memories out of the garbage."

"Val!"

"You've got some nerve asking me for anything. You wanted a clean break. Guess you'll be breaking up with your shit too. Do not call here again."

It took a lot of restraint for Val not to slam the phone down. She took a few deep breaths to tamp down the anger and nausea rising in her throat. She searched the desk for the office phone manual; her next project was blocking Gloria's number.

Perched on a stool in Manfred's Diner, Val didn't need a menu. She wanted The Monster, a half-pound, 100% beef burger drenched in cheddar, bacon, sliced mushrooms, fried onions, and barbeque sauce with fries piled high. Usually, she went for the low carb version--extra lettuce instead of a bun--but tonight, Val wanted to live dangerously.

She would follow it down with two cups of bitter coffee. Perhaps some apple pie. It could take up to two hours to get through the entire meal. To put it simply, Val didn't want to go home.

Nights were almost unbearable. During turbulent dreams, Val instinctively reached out for comfort and was startled awake by cold sheets. From the breakfast nook to the bathroom fixtures, she could see Gloria's influence in the design. It was as if the house itself mocked her.

Rather than face her new reality, Val indulged her taste buds. That was the good thing about New Jersey—you could go to a different diner every night. Each one had its own theme and quirks. The Little Dipper Diner was all politics all the time. The Reuben catered to sports junkies. Thursday found trivia teams competing for clout and free appetizers at Pancake Palace. Manfred, however, was a little more eccentric. His television sets were turned to the latest psychic or supernatural reality show.

Every Tuesday for the last three weeks, Val sat at Manfred's counter ready to make fun of what she called "spook-o-vision." When *Razing the Dead* came on, the owner himself came from behind the cash register and stood transfixed.

Eleanor Razing and her team of paranormal investigators traveled to haunted houses all over the US with hopes of convincing the dead to move on. The show also featured amateurs who claimed unusual psychic abilities--like the plumber who believed spirits were trying to communicate through bathroom tile.

It was brilliant! Eleanor would profile the eccentric first. When she started the investigation, she only gave vague impressions as to what was going on in the spiritual realm. Her slow, measured response sounded reasonable when compared to the antics of a fledgling spiritualists.

Tonight's show featured Clara Janovich, a homemaker who believed worn kitchen floors captured spiritual energy. After espousing her theory, she got on the ground to decipher patterns in the linoleum of a house with a troubled past.

Eleanor kept a straight face throughout the demonstration. Then, while her assistants probed the air with various electronic apparatus, she closed her eyes, lifted a delicate hand to her temple, inhaled deeply, and in a tiny voice announced: "I sense a sadness in this place."

A fit of laughter overtook Val. She nearly choked on a fry. "I can't believe this," she said aloud. "I can do that."

"Are you a sensitive too?" The question came from her right and took Val by surprise. A small, elderly white woman one stool over was staring at her. "Can you talk to the dead?"

"I'm as qualified as anyone on television," Val scoffed.

The woman's eyes lit up. "Do you think you can give me a reading? The waiting list to see Eleanor is so long. I've been trying to contact my husband. Can you sense him around me?"

Oh no, Val thought. "Ma'am, I was being sarcastic. Not towards you, towards the show. I can't talk to the dead."

The senior citizen moved in closer. "I understand how these things work, dear. I believe people should be paid for their spiritual gifts."

Val was amused. "I'm sure there are plenty of people who will take your money, but I'm not one of them. Really, I can't help you." She turned back to the television where Eleanor felt a sudden chill and one of her lackeys thrust an electronic meter towards the camera.

Crestfallen, the woman eased down off her stool and went to the ladies' room.

Sharon, the waitress, came by to refill their coffee cups. "That's Fran. Since Ed died, she's even nuttier than Manfred about this psychic stuff."

"She better be careful," Val said. "A con artist could have a field day with her."

"They already have. She's spent thousands on palm readers and spiritualists. Barbara, her oldest, is threatening to take control of the checkbook. Me? I say leave the dead alone. Ain't nothing they can do for you now anyway."

Fran came back and the three women exchanged sad smiles.

A strange noise had startled Eleanor Razing's crew. They turned on their night-vision goggles and carefully descended into a creepy basement.

Distracted by the antics on screen, Val reached for the sugar. She snatched the last white packet right out from under Fran's grasping fingers. "I'm sorry, I didn't see you. Please, take this. I'll get us more."

"It's Ed," Fran said, her voice trembling. She grabbed Val's arm. "He would move the sugar out of the way, so I'd have to use that fake mess. You can hear him, can't you?"

Manfred uncurled the bony fingers from Val's wrist. "Fran, let the young lady go. She's never even met Ed."

Shaken, Val tried not to show it. She paid at the register, left an overgenerous tip, and dropped her business card in the large fishbowl for the weekly "free meal" drawing. A few miles down the road, her hands finally stopped shaking. She could think of nothing except getting home and crawling into bed next to--damn.

It looked like a filing cabinet had exploded in Val's office. The scattered papers didn't appear to be in any order, but she could find any document within seconds. Now a guest was coming and she needed to clean up fast.

Work had become a welcome distraction. When Val's mind drifted, it went back to the breakup and envisioned possible scenarios that could have kept Gloria from leaving. There was nothing like a contractual review to end daydreams.

The buzzing intercom prompted Val to hide a stack of folders under her desk. Her one thirty appointment, the content manager of SharkStark, was fifteen minutes early. A couple of baby wipes insured that her face and fingers were lunch free. After a quick re-application of lipstick, she was ready.

Her assistant's voice crackled through the speaker. "Ms. Dawson, Mrs. Bowman here to see you."

"Thanks, Serena. Send her in." Flipping open her appointment calendar, Val realized something was off. SharkStark was sending an Alicia Capinelli.

"I'm sorry to trouble you, young lady," said the familiar frail voice, "but I know my Ed is trying to reach me through you."

Val looked up and there stood Mrs. Bowman— Francine Bowman, according to her security pass— in a cream polyester pants suit. "How did--" Before she could finish the question, she remembered the fishbowl full of business cards. I am so stupid.

"Mrs. Bowman, I am not a psychic. If I had known about your loss, I would have kept my mouth shut."

Tears welled up in Fran's eyes and she took a bulging envelope out of her purse. "It's all I have left from Ed's life insurance."

I am in the wrong line of work, Val thought. "I'm sure your husband worked very hard while he was alive to provide for your family. That money is so you can live comfortably, not to give away to strangers."

Crying openly, Fran helped herself to the box of tissues on the desk. "Everybody wants me to get over it. Even our children don't understand. You can't live with someone for forty years and not notice they're gone."

"I know what it's like to lose someone. It's hurtful, but it's best to remember the good parts and move on." With one thirty quickly approaching, Val gently but firmly took the woman's arm and led her to the elevator bank.

"This was supposed to be our time." Fran sniffled and dabbed at her eyes all the way to the ground floor.

Val walked her through the lobby and outside. The next words caught in her throat; she took a deep breath before forcing them out. "It's disorienting to find yourself suddenly alone. Have you tried talking to someone about your grief?"

Fran shrugged. "It's not the same." Her eyes vacant, she wandered out into the thick pedestrian traffic.

Val sighed. She should have offered the older woman a chance to freshen up and calm down before sending her back out in the world. She was about to turn away, when she saw a truck speeding around the corner. Knocking others aside, Val snatched Fran away from the curb just as the truck clipped the sidewalk. "Mrs. Bowman, are you all right?"

Fran responded with a fresh stream of tears. "You saved my life," she whispered. "You knew."

The sudden pull had jostled open Fran's purse and its contents spilled onto the ground. Instinctively, Val reached for the envelope. Under it, she found an aging photo of a young woman dressed like a flapper standing next to an anemic cowboy. She thrust them back into the bag and gave it back to its owner. "Mrs. Bowman, how did you get here? I don't think you're in any condition to drive."

A small group had assembled to shout curses after the truck and make sure Fran was okay. She ignored the strangers fawning over her and locked eyes with Val. "Ed?"

~

Tired and frustrated, Val didn't let it show. She strode across the lobby, ignoring Fran, who had for the fourth straight day set up camp in the Caffeine Hut.

Security captain Chandra Franks was waiting in Val's office. "Is the old lady your girlfriend or what?" Unlike the other members of the security team, she had a reputation for being highly efficient. Behind closed doors with Val, the ultra-professional facade disappeared. "When did you start dating the Geritol set?"

Ignoring the quip, Val pulled a bag of freshly made doughnuts from her tote. "Two chocolate double glazed," she said. "I held up my end of the bargain. Spill it."

After taking a bite of breakfast, Chandra put it

aside and took a notepad from her breast pocket. "She gets to Caffeine Hut at about eight and orders a large mocha latte and biscotti. She sits at the table all day, reading a newspaper, doing crosswords, whatever. Her eyes are glued to you every second you are in the lobby. She leaves when you do." Chandra closed the book and reached for a doughnut. "Why is this woman stalking you?"

"She's convinced I have a connection to her dead husband."

"What kind of connection? Like you're his long-lost daughter or something?"

"A psychic link," Val said. "She thinks I can communicate with him from beyond the grave."

Chandra raised an eyebrow. "You see dead people?"

"No, but she swears her husband is trying to reach her through me. Want to hear something funny? I did my own Google investigation and found his obituary. His name was Ernest Daniel Bowman; he died eighteen months ago at the age of ninety-two. He married his childhood sweetheart and had a series of jobs - bit actor, shoe salesman, insurance man - before settling into real estate."

"Childhood sweetheart? Francine Bowman is not in her 90s."

Val shrugged. "I didn't say they were the same age. Want to hear something funny? His name sounds familiar, but I don't know why."

Chandra hummed the theme from the *Twilight Zone*. "Maybe the old lady is right. You do kinda look like Whoopi Goldberg."

"Don't play." Val tossed her locs back and rolled her eyes. "This woman has offered me money. She needs to be stopped. I wouldn't be surprised if she's sitting at my desk tomorrow."

The guard suddenly became serious. "Mrs. Bowman should never have made it beyond the lobby. Guests visiting the third floor and higher are supposed to have a verifiable appointment. Since she wasn't on a pre-approved list, Officer Powell should have called your secretary to confirm. He's been disciplined and all guards have been reminded of visitor procedures." Chandra shook her head. "She won't get up here again."

"Can you ban her from the building?"

"Even though the woman makes you feel

uncomfortable, she hasn't actually done anything illegal. My guards don't have time to scrutinize every white-haired senior in a psychedelic suit; there is a podiatrist office on the ground floor."

"What if I got a restraining order?"

"Girl, the courts aren't going to take you seriously. Why don't you take a few days off? Maybe not seeing you for a few days will make her go away."

Val put her head in her hands. How had she gone from avoiding one woman to hiding from two? "No, I need to put a stop to this now."

"Whatever you do, don't lose your cool. She automatically wins sympathy for being old. If you yell at her, she's going to look like the victim."

"So you're saying I can't win?"

"Basically."

~

After fortifying herself with office brew, Val headed to the Caffeine Hut for a gentle confrontation. She sat across from Fran, who jumped in surprise. "You startled me. I didn't see you coming."

"Well," Val said, "I guess that means neither of us is psychic."

"You have to help me," Fran pleaded. Her eyes filled with tears. "Being near you, I can feel him. Have you ever lost someone before you had a chance to apologize?"

After a few minutes of staring at empty creamers, Val decided to try a different approach. "What would your daughter think about you trying to give money away to strangers?"

Fran shook her head vigorously. "No! You can't tell Barbara."

A few heads had turned, so Val put on her best, comforting smile. "Then leave me alone, Mrs. Bowman. I hope you do get the help you need, but I'm not the one."

Fran wiped her eyes, packed up her magazines, and left. Val tried to imagine forty years of living with a woman who had to have everything her way. Even if he was dancing on pitchforks, Ed was probably in a better place.

Gloria is too. The thought came out of nowhere

and Val suddenly felt sick. Mrs. Bowman wasn't the only one who needed to let go of the past. She dialed her ex. Of course, the call went straight to voicemail. "Gloria, this is your last chance. This Saturday, I'll be out from 10 am to noon. The storm door will be unlocked and alarm off. That should give you plenty of time to get your stuff."

A Caffeine Hut employee hovered near the table with a dishtowel. Val got the hint; it was literally time to move on.

~

Reed's Express didn't quite live up to its name on weekends. The line snaking around the popular breakfast spot moved but never got smaller. Rather than wait for a spot to open at the counter, Val got her Belgian waffle with country bacon to go. It was lukewarm when she stopped to eat at a park bench, but every bite of waffle was drenched in melted butter.

A decent breakfast with a goodnight's sleep made Val feel a little stronger. She was ready to start dealing with her emotions. A notification on her phone let her know that the front door had been opened. Gloria was following through on her desire to totally separate.

One thing was certain, there was no chance to rekindle a romantic relationship. Val could concede that she had been neglectful, but she deserved better than a disappearing act. Even if Gloria wanted to reconcile, she could never trust her again. Was it too late to salvage a friendship? Val wasn't sure if she wanted one.

Thirty minutes later, Val realized she hadn't received any more notifications from her alarm app. The front door was still wide open. Could Gloria have changed her mind and be moving furniture? Giving her a two-hour window was a mistake. Val needed to get back home.

A familiar Prius was in the driveway; there was no moving van in sight. Unsure of her ex-lover's intentions, Val decided she would announce her presence and retreat to the kitchen. She imagined any attempt at a relationship post-mortem devolving into a screaming match.

Approaching the open front door, Val saw a sickly Gloria on the sofa. She looked horrible. Was the breakup wearing her down? Val felt a surge of joy, though it was almost instantly tempered with pangs of guilt.

When Gloria saw Val, she shook her head and

mouthed "no."

It was too late. Val stepped into the living room and saw Fran sitting in the loveseat. The grieving widow had a gun. "What you're doing is a sin," she said. "People like you are just selfish. When God gives you a talent, you are supposed to use it."

Too shocked to be afraid, Val yelled, "I am not a psychic!" *Did this woman follow me home?*

Fran snorted. "Then explain the elevators."

"What are you talking about?"

"I've been watching you. There are six elevators in your building and you always know which one to stand in front of before it arrives."

Val didn't know whether to laugh or cry. This woman was psychotic. There was nothing she could say or do to convince her of the truth.

Gloria's hands were shaking, but her voice was calm. "Valerie, what's going on? Fran has been telling me about sugar and dead cowboys."

Val started to go over to Gloria. "Baby, it's-"

"Oh no," Fran said, waving the gun at both. "You don't get to talk to her until I speak to Ed."

Gloria nodded. "Give her what she wants. It's been a while, but I'm sure you can do it." She didn't move, but her eyes swept from Val to the open door. "You have to do this."

For the first time in a year, they were communicating clearly. Val immediately set out to distract Fran so Gloria could get help. "Okay, Mrs. Bowman. You win." She walked directly into the path of the gun. "I don't know the future and the dead only talk to me when their loved ones are near."

In her peripheral vision, she could see Gloria rising from the chair. Fran saw it too, but Val put up her hand. "I won't work under duress. She has to be safe before I let Ed come through."

Fran inched forward in her seat. "Don't shit me. Give me a sign that you are really talking to my Ed."

As she stared into the barrel of the six-shooter, Val's mind felt like it was about to explode. "Ernest Daniel Bowman, can you hear me?" Fran gasped at the mention of her husband's full name.

While Gloria slipped out, Val desperately combed her memories. Why did she know that name? A chain of ideas rapidly flowed through her consciousness: six-shooter, cowboys, cattle rustlers. . . Suddenly, she remembered western night at Pancake Palace. Ernest Daniel Bowman was the answer to a trivia question: Who played local Saturday morning host Cowboy Ed?

No one got the correct answer, but the trivia master taught them the show theme song. Now the words tumbled from Val's lips. "Sleepy head, it's time to get out of bed, watch your cartoon favorites with Cowboy Ed."

Shocked, Fran lowered the gun. "Oh my, God, " she whispered. "He's here."

Val hoped her Eleanor Razing impression would be enough to carry her through. "Ed is with you. He's always with you, but you know this. You refuse to see." She paused for dramatic effect. "He says you weren't trying to find him--you were trying to lose him?"

Fran's eyes filled with terror. "What is he saying about me? I have to know."

"You can't hear him because you are afraid, but—" Val's legs buckled and she reached out to steady herself on the sofa. "I feel dizzy." The next time she "stumbled," she was going to try to wrestle the gun away.

"Ed, it was an accident," Fran said, her eyes darting around the room. "I didn't know you were hurt until I saw the blood."

The hair on the back of Val's neck stood up. "Of course he forgives you. He's lonely, Mrs. Bowman. He misses you." Swallowing hard, Val got into position to lunge. "Mrs. Bowman, I'm losing him...he's getting faint."

"Ed, no!" Fran put the barrel in her mouth and pulled the trigger. There was a click, but no shot. Screaming, she dropped the gun and ran outside.

Careful not to touch it, Val took a closer look at the weapon. The damn thing had been empty the whole time. Sirens blared in the distance.

Walking out on the porch, Val took stock of the situation. Fran paced back and forth along the gravel driveway crying to a husband no one could see. Phone in hand, Gloria waved down an approaching ambulance. Neighbors peeked from behind curtains.

Val sat on the top step, closed her eyes, and

enjoyed the afternoon breeze. It was over.

Everything was over...and she was going to be fine.